GRAVEYARD RATS
AND OTHERS

ALSO BY ROBERT E. HOWARD

Waterfront Fists and Others

GRAVEYARD RATS AND OTHERS

ROBERT E. HOWARD

Introduction by Don Herron

Edited by Paul Herman

WILDSIDE PRESS
MMIII

GRAVEYARD RATS AND OTHERS

"Black Talons" first appeared in *Strange Detective Stories*, December 1933.
"Fangs Of Gold" first appeared in *Strange Detective Stories*, February 1934.
"The Tomb's Secret" first appeared in *Strange Detective Stories*, February 1934.
"Names in The Black Book" first appeared in *Super-Detective Stories*, May 1934. "Graveyard Rats" first appeared in *Thrilling Mystery*, February 1936.
"Black Wind Blowing" first appeared in *Thrilling Mystery*, June 1936.

Published by
Wildside Press
P.O. Box 301
Holicong, PA 18928-0301 USA
www.wildsidepress.com

CONTENTS

A BLACK WIND
OFF RIVER STREET

Don Herron

An abiding mystery of Robert E. Howard's volcanic career as a
writer for the wood pulp fiction magazines remains: Why he didn't
smoke the keys on his Underwood with one hard-boiled detective
story after another?

Howard had the speed, the influences, the personal interest in
guns and boxing and other hallmarks of the tough guy crime tale. He
hit his professional stride in exactly the right era. Among the vast
hosts of his fellow fictioneers, Howard was one of the few to create an
enduring icon of the hard-boiled attitude of his age with his most popular creation, Conan: a character and a mood, tougher than tough.

Nailed to the cross in "A Witch Shall be Born," the Cimmerian
emerges triumphant from the ordeal, a quintessential image torn from
the heart of the Great Depression. If the American readership of *Weird
Tales*, from young teens on up, needed reassurance that adversity could
be met, Howard gave it to them in mythic terms told in emotionally
immediate prose. You want a tough guy who can survive anything
thrown at him, *here's* your tough guy.

Of course, most *Weird Tales* readers probably weren't looking at the
story with quite those ideas in mind. It usually takes a little time for
this kind of evaluation to shake out. When the Dime Novels of the
1800s were trying on various character types, looking for The Hero
whose exploits would sell copy after copy, it wasn't evident immedi-
ately that The Cowboy was the archetype which would survive and
dominate much of American pop culture in the Twentieth Century.

You cannot say with certainty that Howard himself had a single clue that he had created The Barbarian, not merely a few characters in a fairly large group of stories, but yet another archetype that would ease out into world culture over the next half-century. Yet Robert E. Howard and no one else created The Barbarian in the same era in which another new archetype came along to give The Cowboy a serious challenge as America's dominant pop culture hero. Both The Barbarian and The Private Eye were born in the wood pulp magazines of the 1920s and 1930s.

Howard came so close to the tone, setting and concerns of the hard-boiled Private Eye story, it is astonishing that he managed to keep to his own path and carve out a new genre of fiction with his tales of Sword-and-Sorcery. The scenes with Shevatas the thief in the Conan yarn "Black Colossus" or with Conan himself as a young thief in "The Tower of the Elephant" play with the materials of the pulp crime story. Without any need for qualification, "Rogues in the House" is one of the best hard-boiled stories of the era, featuring terrific moments such as the jailer who "had become careless in his dealings with the underworld" or Conan tossing "his punk" who had betrayed him into a cesspool. Especially hard-boiled is the casual thought, when the barbarian "decided it was time for him to kill Nabonidus."

So close, yet only a month before his death by suicide in June 1936, Howard would tell H. P. Lovecraft in a letter that he could "scarcely endure to read" a detective story, "much less write one."

In 1935 the Texan briefed Clark Ashton Smith, another of his peers in the pages of *Weird Tales*, on the creation of Conan: "It may sound fantastic to link the term 'realism' with Conan; but as a matter of fact—his supernatural adventures aside—he is the most realistic character I ever evolved. He is simply a combination of a number of men I have known. . . . Some mechanism in my sub-consciousness took the dominant characteristics of various prize-fighters, gunmen, bootleggers, oil field bullies, gamblers, and honest workmen I had come in contact with, and combining them all, produced the amalgamation I call Conan the Cimmerian." Gunmen and gamblers, bootleggers and prize-fighters—the solid stuff of hard-boiled fiction.

Howard's taste in movies underlines his innate attraction to the form: "Give me a rough, tough brutal story, quick action and a gang of hard-boiled hairy chested eggs: George Bancroft; Mathew Betz; Lionel Barrymore; Vic Maclaglen, who once fought Jack Johnson. . . ." If any writer was participating in the cultural moment, that writer was Robert E. Howard.

The first World War brought literature and film to the boil, although other forces had set out simmering fires earlier. The rise of literary naturalism in the late Nineteenth Century paved the way for a brand of tough-minded realism, and one of Howard's favorite authors, Jack London, dead at age forty in 1916, was a significant factor in popularizing what would become known as "tough guy" writing. But it took a world actually going to war to set in motion the social and economic forces that would bring the detective story up to speed. Edgar Allan Poe had inaugurated the detective and mystery genre with "Murders in the Rue Morgue" in 1841, with Arthur Conan Doyle's private investigator Sherlock Holmes the most enduringly popular figure to emerge from the hundreds of fictional detectives to trail in Poe's wake. Still, before the war, crime fiction lacked a convincing sense of what was realistic.

The realistic hard-boiled form exploded out of the postwar pulps, specifically *The Black Mask*, which began publication in 1920, though it wasn't until October 1922 that the significant creative fires were lit. In that issue you find "The Road Home," the first detective story by

Dashiell Hammett, the unquestioned modern master, as well as "The False Burton Combs" by Carroll John Daly, a lesser figure but nonetheless a major influence on later writers such as Mickey Spillane. Daly rapidly produced more stories featuring tough-talking private eyes, but we can look back now and see that it was in 1923 when the hard-boiled detective arrived to stay. That year Hammett began his long series of short stories, novelettes and novels about the exploits of an unnamed operative for the Continental Detective Agency with a tale called "Arson Plus." By 1928, when Hammett began writing his novel *The Maltese Falcon*, few had any doubts that something new, something great, had come to literature.

Robert E. Howard's major market for fiction, *Weird Tales*, also was born in 1923, and the teenaged Howard managed to place three stories with that magazine by 1924. He came into the fiction magazine scene virtually on Hammett's heels. It's interesting to note that the next major hard-boiled crime writer after Hammett, Raymond Chandler, first appeared in the pages of *Black Mask* in the December 1933 issue with "Blackmailers Don't Shoot." By that time Howard himself was a full-fledged professional writer; he had created Conan in 1932.

In that specific period in the pulps, from no earlier than 1922, with no need to go any later than 1936, the year of Howard's death, a number of writers following Hammett's lead hard-boiled the detective story. While they did that, Howard single-handed performed the same job for the fantastic tale, imbuing his stories with the tough realism of the day, adding a new dimension to otherworldly fantasy.

If some hardcore Howard enthusiasts may be experiencing a strong sense of *déjà vû* by this point, perhaps it's because I have made this argument at length before, some twenty years ago. In 1984 for *The Dark Barbarian*, a critical anthology about Howard's writing I edited, I wrote an essay on this theme entitled "Robert E. Howard: Hard-Boiled Heroic Fantasist." Since I also wrote the essay "The Dark Barbarian" for that book, I decided to disguise the hard-boiled section a bit by using the *nom-de-plume* "George Knight." In part I did that for fun, and the fact was that in 1984 you didn't have Robert E. Howard critics falling out of the trees—not like today. If I wanted that essay, and I did, then I had to write it myself.

So, you can see that I've been intrigued by the problem of Howard largely missing out on the most fecund and significant era of the hard-boiled detective story for quite a long time. As a big fan of both Hammett and Howard, this situation gnaws at me. What if? Why didn't it happen? Wonderful questions.

This collection demonstrates, however, that Howard did not miss his chance completely. A working professional, willing to try any marketplace to make a living, he swallowed his aversion to the detective formula and wrote these tales during the years he chronicled the adventures of Conan. At the same time, he was writing his boxing stories and becoming increasingly interested in Westerns, both serious sagebrushers and his popular burlesques featuring such Tall Tale heroes as Breckinridge Elkins. If he had lived—another always arresting What If—surely Howard would have done more detective stories. And if these stories aren't on a par with the best of Hammett and Chandler, they're not much worse than many other yarns published in that heyday of the hard-boiled—I've actually met people who *like* Carroll John Daly's stories, for some reason.

Howard clearly sensed how to shape his backdrop, although he didn't do quite enough with detective tales to start filling it all in. You have a private eye named Steve Harrison—or more than one private eye named Steve Harrison—and you have a mysterious locale called River Street: "It was absurd to suppose that the dead Mongol fiend was behind these murderous attacks, yet—Harrison's flesh crawled along his spine at the memory of things that had taken place in River Street—things he had never reported, because he did not wish to be thought either a liar or a madman. The dead do not return—but what seems absurd on Thirty-ninth Boulevard takes on a different aspect among the haunted labyrinths of the Oriental quarter." Yeah, that River Street setting, where "three unsolved murders in a week are not so unusual," could have been a real hotbed for some hard-boiled detective action.

The least stories here perhaps are "Black Talons" and "Fangs of Gold," replete with virulent racism and xenophobia, but then racism and xenophobia were common in that era and pulp marketplace. If ethically deplorable, an equally strong objection may be made that Howard doesn't make these stories stand up and rock—which he does with much the same material in his horror story "Black Canaan."

"Names in the Black Book" impresses me as being equal to several of the escapades Howard wrote about El Borak, adventuring in the wild, rocky hills of Afghanistan. Paul Herman, the editor for this collection, feels that Howard was starting to hit his stride with "Graveyard Rats." I must agree—he reaches a fever pitch of fear that places this one on a par with the story of the same title by Henry Kuttner, while playing fair with the conventions of the crime story.

And may I point out that a quick glance at the content's page will remind you of the fact that Howard often used the word "black" (and "dark," as well) in his titles—as I was saying twenty years ago in "The Dark Barbarian," that's because these words represent Howard's *content and themes*, not for any lack of inventiveness on his part.

If Howard did not do much with the detective story, he left us with at least this much—and in the larger hard-boiled arena of his day, he was a giant figure. I'd place his Conan saga against Hammett's Continental Op series any day—both have a few weaker entries, yet both have one story after another that still burn with that same white-hot fire that shrouded the pages as they rolled off the typewriter. Against such poetic masterpieces as Chandler's "Red Wind" you might pit Howard's "Worms of the Earth." Hammett, Howard, Chandler—they are among the finest writers to emerge from the pulps.

And if it's too damn bad that Howard never managed to get going with hard-boiled detective tales, I have another thought: wouldn't it have been fascinating if Dashiell Hammett had tried his hand at the Sword-and-Sorcery tale? Great, bad, indifferent, but enough to fill a book of this size?

BLACK TALONS

Joel Brill slapped shut the book he had been scanning, and gave vent to his dissatisfaction in language more appropriate for the deck of a whaling ship than for the library of the exclusive Corinthian Club. Buckley, seated in an alcove nearby, grinned quietly. Buckley looked more like a college professor than a detective, and perhaps it was less because of a studious nature than a desire to play the part he looked, that caused him to loaf around the library of the Corinthian.

"It must be something unusual to drag you out of your lair at this time of the day," he remarked. "This is the first time I ever saw you in the evening. I thought you spent your evenings secluded in your rooms, pouring over musty tomes in the interests of that museum you're connected with."

"I do, ordinarily." Brill looked as little like a scientist as Buckley looked like a dick. He was squarely built, with thick shoulders and the jaw and fists of a prizefighter; low browed, with a mane of tousled black hair contrasting with his cold blue eyes.

"You've been shoving your nose into books here since six o'clock," asserted Buckley.

"I've been trying to get some information for the directors of the museum," answered Brill. "Look!" He pointed an accusing finger at the rows of lavishly bound volumes. "Books till it would sicken a dog—and not a blasted one can tell me the reason for a certain ceremonial dance practiced by a certain tribe on the West African Coast."

"A lot of the members have knocked around a bit," suggested Buckley. "Why not ask them?"

"I'm going to." Brill took down a phone from its hook.

"There's John Galt—" began Buckley.

"Too hard to locate. He flits about like a mosquito with the St. Vitus. I'll try Jim Reynolds." He twirled the dial.

"Thought you'd done some exploring in the tropics yourself," remarked Buckley.

"Not worthy of the name. I hung around that God-forsaken Hell hole of the West African Coast for a few months until I came down with malaria—Hello!"

A suave voice, too perfectly accented, came along the wire.

"Oh, is that you, Yut Wuen? I want to speak to Mr. Reynolds."

Polite surprise tinged the meticulous tone.

"Why, Mr. Reynolds went out in response to your call an hour ago, Mr. Brill."

"What's that?" demanded Brill. "Went where?"

"Why, surely you remember, Mr. Brill." A faint uneasiness seemed to edge the Chinaman's voice. "At about nine o'clock you called, and I answered the phone. You said you wished to speak to Mr. Reynolds. Mr. Reynolds talked to you, then told me to have his car brought around to the side entrance. He said that you had requested him to meet you at the cottage on White Lake shore."

"Nonsense!" exclaimed Brill. "This is the first time I've phoned Reynolds for weeks! You've mistaken somebody else for me."

There was no reply, but a polite stubbornness seemed to flow over the wire. Brill replaced the phone and turned to Buckley, who was leaning forward with aroused interest.

"Something fishy here," scowled Brill. "Yut Wuen, Jim's Chinese servant, said *I* called, an hour ago, and Jim went out to meet me. Buckley, you've been here all evening. *Did* I call up anybody? I'm so infernally absent-minded—"

"No, you didn't," emphatically answered the detective. "I've been sitting right here close to the phone ever since six o'clock. Nobody's used it. And you haven't left the library during that time. I'm so accustomed to spying on people, I do it unconsciously."

"Well, say," said Brill, uneasily, "suppose you and I drive over to White Lake. If this is a joke, Jim may be over there waiting for me to show up."

As the city lights fell behind them, and houses gave way to clumps of trees and bushes, velvet black in the star-light, Buckley said: "Do you think Yut Wuen made a mistake?"

"What else could it be?" answered Brill, irritably.

"Somebody might have been playing a joke, as you suggested. Why should anybody impersonate you to Reynolds?"

"How should I know? But I'm about the only acquaintance he'd bestir himself for, at this time of night. He's reserved, suspicious of people. Hasn't many friends. I happen to be one of the few."

"Something of a traveler, isn't he?"

"There's no corner of the world with which he isn't familiar."

"How'd he make his money?" Buckley asked, abruptly.

"I've never asked him. But he has plenty of it."

The clumps on each side of the road grew denser, and scattered pinpoints of light that marked isolated farm houses faded out behind them. The road tilted gradually as they climbed higher and higher into the wild hill region which, an hour's drive from the city, locked the broad crystalline sheet of silver that men called White Lake. Now ahead of them a glint shivered among the trees, and topping a wooded crest, they saw the lake spread out below them, reflecting the stars in myriad flecks of silver. The road meandered along the curving shore.

"Where's Reynolds' lodge?" inquired Buckley.

Brill pointed. "See that thick clump of shadows, within a few yards of the water's edge? It's the only cottage on this side of the lake. The others are three or four miles away. None of them occupied, this time of the year. There's a car drawn up in front of the cottage."

"No light in the shack," grunted Buckley, pulling up beside the long low roadster that stood before the narrow stoop. The building reared dark and silent before them, blocked against the rippling silver sheen behind it.

"Hey, Jim!" called Brill. "Jim Reynolds!"

No answer. Only a vague echo shuddering down from the blackly wooded hills.

"Devil of a place at night," muttered Buckley, peering at the dense shadows that bordered the lake. "We might be a thousand miles from civilization."

Brill slid out of the car. "Reynolds must be here—unless he's gone for a midnight boat ride."

Their steps echoed loudly and emptily on the tiny stoop. Brill banged the door and shouted. Somewhere back in the woods a night bird lifted a drowsy note. There was no other answer.

Buckley shook the door. It was locked from the inside.

"I don't like this," he growled. "Car in front of the cottage—door locked on the inside—nobody answering it. I believe I'll break the door in—"

"No need." Brill fumbled in his pocket. "I'll use my key."

"How comes it you have a key to Reynolds' shack?" demanded Buckley.

"It was his own idea. I spent some time with him up here last summer, and he insisted on giving me a key, so I could use the cottage any time I wanted to. Turn on your flash, will you? I can't find the lock. All right, I've got it. Hey, Jim! Are you here?"

Buckley's flash played over chairs and card tables, coming to rest on a closed door in the opposite wall. They entered and Buckley heard Brill fumbling about with an arm elevated. A faint click followed and Brill swore.

"The juice is off. There's a line running out from town to supply the cottage owners with electricity, but it must be dead. As long as we're in here, let's go through the house. Reynolds may be sleeping somewhere—"

He broke off with a sharp intake of breath. Buckley had opened the door that led to the bedroom. His flash played on the interior—on a broken chair, a smashed table—a crumpled shape that lay in the midst of a dark widening pool.

"Good God, it's Reynolds!"

Buckley's gun glinted in his hand as he played the flash around the room, sifting the shadows for lurking shapes of menace; it rested on a bolted rear door; rested longer on an open window, the screen of which hung in tatters.

"We've got to have more light," he grunted. "Where's the switch? Maybe a fuse has blown."

"Outside, near that window." Stumblingly Brill led the way out of the house and around to the window. Buckley flashed his light, grunted.

"The switch has been pulled!" He pushed it back in place, and light flooded the cottage. The light streaming through the windows seemed to emphasize the blackness of the whispering woods around them. Buckley glared into the shadows, seemed to shiver. Brill had not spoken; he shook as with ague.

Back in the house they bent over the man who lay in the middle of the red-splashed floor.

Jim Reynolds had been a stocky, strongly built man of middle age. His skin was brown and weather-beaten, hinting of tropic suns. His features were masked with blood; his head lolled back, disclosing an awful wound beneath his chin.

"His throat's been cut!" stammered Brill. Buckley shook his head.

"Not cut—torn. Good God, it looks like a big cat had ripped him."

The whole throat had literally been torn out; muscles, arteries, windpipe and the great jugular vein had been severed; the bones of the vertebrae showed beneath.

"He's so bloody I wouldn't have recognized him," muttered the detective. "How did you know him so quickly? The instant we saw him, you cried out that it was Reynolds."

"I recognized his garments and his build," answered the other. "But what in God's name killed him?"

Buckley straightened and looked about. "Where does that door lead to?"

"To the kitchen; but it's locked on this side."

"And the outer door of the front room was locked on the inside," muttered Buckley. "Doesn't take a genius to see how the murderer got in—and he—or *it*—went out the same way."

"What do you mean, *it?*"

"Does that look like the work of a human being?" Buckley pointed to the dead man's mangled throat. Brill winced.

"I've seen black boys mauled by the big cats on the West Coast—"

"And whatever tore Reynolds' gullet out, tore that window screen. It wasn't cut with a knife."

"Do you suppose a panther from the hills—" began Brill.

"A panther smart enough to throw the electric switch before he slid through the window?" scoffed Buckley.

"We don't know the killer threw the switch."

"Was Reynolds fooling around in the dark, then? No; when I pushed the switch back in place, the light came on in here. That shows it had been on; the button hadn't been pushed back. Whoever killed Reynolds had a reason for wanting to work in the dark. Maybe this was it!" The detective indicated, with a square-shod toe, a stubby chunk of blue steel that lay not far from the body.

"From what I hear about Reynolds, he was quick enough on the trigger." Buckley slipped on a glove, carefully lifted the revolver, and scanned the chamber. His gaze, roving about the room again, halted at the window, and with a single long stride, he reached it and bent over the sill.

"One shot's been fired from this gun. The bullet's in the window sill. At least, one bullet is, and it's logical to suppose it's the one from the empty chamber of Reynolds' gun. Here's the way I reconstruct the crime: *something* sneaked up to the shack, threw the switch, and came busting through the window. Reynolds shot once in the dark and missed, and then the killer got in his work. I'll take this gun to head-quarters; don't expect to find any fingerprints except Reynolds', how-ever. We'll examine the light switch, too, though maybe my dumb pawing erased any fingerprints that might have been there. Say, it's a good thing you have an iron-clad alibi."

Brill started violently. "What the Hell do you mean?"

"Why, there's the Chinaman to swear you called Reynolds to his death."

"Why the devil should I do such a thing?" hotly demanded the sci-entist.

"Well," answered Buckley, "I know you were in the library of the club all evening. That's an unshakable alibi—I suppose."

Brill was tired as he locked the door of his garage and turned toward the house which rose dark and silent among the trees. He found himself wishing that his sister, with whom be was staying, had not left town for the weekend with her husband and children. Dark empty houses were vaguely repellent to him after the happenings of the night before.

He sighed wearily as he trudged toward the house, under the dense shadows of the trees that lined the driveway. It had been a morbid, and harrying day. Tag ends of thoughts and worries flitted through his mind. Uneasily he remembered Buckley's cryptic remark: "Either Yut Wuen is lying about that telephone call, or—" The detective had left the sentence unfinished, casting a glance at Brill that was as inscrutable as his speech. Nobody believed the Chinaman was deliberately lying. His devotion to his master was well known—a devotion shared by the other servants of the dead man. Police suspicion had failed to connect them in any way with the crime. Apparently none of them had left Reynolds' town house during the day or the night of the murder. Nor had the murder-cottage given up any clues. No tracks had been found on the hard earth, no fingerprints on the gun other than the dead man's nor any except Buckley's on the light switch. If Buckley had had any luck in trying to trace the mysterious phone call, he had not divulged anything.

Brill remembered, with a twinge of nervousness, the way in which they had looked at him, those inscrutable Orientals. Their features had been immobile, but in their dark eyes had gleamed suspicion and a threat. He had seen it in the eyes of Yut Wuen, the stocky yellow man; of Ali, the Egyptian, a lean, sinewy statue of bronze; of Jugra Singh, the tall, broad shouldered, turbaned Sikh. They had not spoken their thoughts; but their eyes had followed him, hot and burning, like beasts of prey.

Brill turned from the meandering driveway to cut across the lawn. As he passed under the black shadow of the trees, something sudden, clinging and smothering, enveloped his head, and steely arms locked fiercely about him. His reaction was as instinctive and violent as that of a trapped leopard. He exploded into a galvanized burst of frantic action, a bucking heave that tore the stifling cloak from his head, and freed his arms from the arms that pinioned him. But another pair of arms hung like grim Fate to his legs, and figures surged in on him from the darkness. He could not tell the nature of his assailants; they were like denser, moving shadows in the blackness.

Staggering, fighting for balance, he lashed out blindly, felt the jolt of a solid hit shoot up his arm, and saw one of the shadows sway and pitch backward. His other arm was caught in a savage grasp and twisted up behind his back so violently that he felt as if the tendons were being ripped from their roots. Hot breath hissed in his ear, and bending his head forward, he jerked it backward again with all the power of his thick neck muscles. He felt the back of his skull crash into something softer—a man's face. There was a groan, and the crippling grip on his imprisoned arm relaxed. With a desperate wrench he tore away, but the arms that clung to his legs tripped him. He pitched headlong, spreading his arms to break his fall, and even before his fingers touched the ground, something exploded in his brain, showering a suddenly starless night of blackness with red sparks that were engulfed abruptly in formless oblivion.

Joel Brill's first conscious thought was that be was being tossed about in an open boat on a stormy sea. Then as his dazed mind cleared, be realized that he was lying in an automobile which was speeding along an uneven road. His head throbbed; he was bound hand and foot, and blanketed in some kind of a cloak. He could see nothing; could hear nothing but the purr of the racing motor. Bewilderment clouded his mind as be sought for a clue to the identity of the kidnappers. Then a sudden suspicion brought out the cold sweat on his skin.

The car lurched to a halt. Powerful hands lifted him, cloak and all, and he felt himself being carried over a short stretch of level ground, and apparently up a step or so. A key grated in a lock, a door rasped on its hinges. Those carrying him advanced; there was a click, and light shone through the folds of the cloth over Brill's head. He felt himself being lowered onto what felt like a bed. Then the cloth was ripped away, and he blinked in the glare of the light. A cold premonitory shudder passed over him.

He was lying on the bed in the room in which James Reynolds had died. And about him stood, arms folded, three grim and silent shapes: Yut Wuen, Ali the Egyptian, and Jugra Singh. There was dried blood on the Chinaman's yellow face, and his lip was cut. A dark blue bruise showed on Jugra Singh's jaw.

"The *sahib* awakes," said the Sikh, in his perfect English.

"What the devil's the idea, Jugra?" demanded Brill, trying to struggle to a sitting posture. "What do you mean by this? Take these ropes off me—" His voice trailed away, a shaky resonance of futility as he read the meaning in the hot dark eyes that regarded him.

"In this room our master met his doom," said Ali.

"*You* called him forth," said Yut Wuen.

"But I didn't!" raged Brill, jerking wildly at the cords which cut into his flesh. "Damn it, I knew nothing about it!"

"Your voice came over the wire and our master followed it to his death," said Jugra Singh.

A panic of helplessness swept over Joel Brill. He felt like a man beating at an insurmountable wall—the wall of inexorable Oriental fatalism, of conviction unchangeable. If even Buckley believed that somehow he, Joel Brill, was connected with Reynolds' death, how was he to convince these immutable Orientals? He fought down an impulse to hysteria.

"The detective, Buckley, was with me all evening," he said, in a voice unnatural from his efforts at control. "He has told you that he did not see me touch a phone; nor did I leave his sight. I could not have killed my friend, your master, because while he was being killed, I was either in the library of the Corinthian Club, or driving from there with Buckley."

"How it was done, we do not know," answered the Sikh, tranquilly. "The ways of the *sahibs* are beyond us. But we *know* that somehow, in some manner, you caused our master's death. And we have brought you here to expiate your crime."

"You mean to murder me?" demanded Brill, his flesh crawling.

"If a *sahib* judge sentenced you, and a *sahib* hangman dropped you through a black trap, white men would call it execution. So it is execution we work upon you, not murder."

Brill opened his mouth, then closed it, realizing the utter futility of argument. The whole affair was like a fantastic nightmare from which he would presently awaken.

Ali came forward with something, the sight of which shook Brill with a nameless foreboding. It was a wire cage, in which a great gaunt rat squealed and bit at the wires. Yut Wuen laid upon a card table a copper bowl, furnished with a slot on each side of the rim, to one of which was made fast a long leather strap. Brill turned suddenly sick.

"These are the tools of execution, *sahib*," said Jugra Singh, somberly. "That bowl shall be laid on your naked belly, the strap drawn about your body and made fast so that the bowl shall not slip. Inside the bowl the rat will be imprisoned. He is ravenous with hunger, wild with fear and rage. For a while he will only run about the bowl, treading on your flesh. But with irons hot from the fire, we shall gradually heat the bowl, until, driven by pain, the rat begins to gnaw his way *out*. He can not gnaw through copper; he can gnaw through flesh—through flesh and muscles and intestines and bones, *sahib*."

Brill wet his lips three times before he found voice to speak.

"You'll hang for this!" he gasped, in a voice he did not himself recognize.

"If it be the will of Allah," assented Ali calmly. "This is your fate; what ours is, no man can say. It is the will of Allah that you die with a rat in your bowels. If it is Allah's will, we shall die on the gallows. Only Allah knows."

Brill made no reply. Some vestige of pride still remained to him. He set his jaw hard, feeling that if he opened his mouth to speak, to reason, to argue, he would collapse into shameful shrieks and entreaties. One was useless as the other, against the abysmal fatalism of the Orient.

Ali set the cage with its grisly Occupant on the table beside the copper bowl—without warning the light went out.

In the darkness Brill's heart began to pound suffocatingly. The Orientals stood still, patiently, expecting the light to come on again. But Brill instinctively felt that the stage was set for some drama darker and more hideous than that which menaced him. Silence reigned; somewhere off in the woods a night bird lifted a drowsy note. There was a faint scratching sound, somewhere—

"The electric torch," muttered a ghostly voice which Brill recognized as Jugra Singh's. "I laid it on the card table. Wait!"

He heard the Sikh fumbling in the dark; but he was watching the window, a square of dim, star-flecked sky blocked out of blackness. And as Brill watched, he saw something dark and bulky rear up in that square. Etched against the stars he saw a misshapen head, vague monstrous shoulders.

A scream sounded from inside the room, the crash of a wildly thrown missile. On the instant there was a scrambling sound, and the object blotted out the square of starlight, then vanished from it. *It was inside the room.*

Brill, lying frozen in his cords, heard all Hell and bedlam break loose in that dark room. Screams, shouts, strident cries of agony mingled with the smashing of furniture, the impact of blows, and a hideous, worrying, tearing sound that made Brill's flesh crawl. Once the battling pack staggered past the window, but Brill made out only a dim writhing of limbs, the pale glint of steel, and the terrible blaze of a pair of eyes he knew belonged to none of his three captors.

Somewhere a man was moaning horribly, his gasps growing weaker and weaker. There was a last convulsion of movement, the groaning impact of a heavy body; then the starlight in the window was for an instant blotted out again, and silence reigned once more in the cottage on the lake shore; silence broken only by the death gasps in the dark, and the labored panting of a wounded man.

Brill heard some one stumbling and floundering in the darkness, and it was from this one that the racking, panting was emanating. A circle of light flashed on, and in it Brill saw the blood-smeared face of Jugra Singh.

The light wandered erratically away, dancing crazily about the walls. Brill heard the Sikh blundering across the room, moving like a drunken man, or like one wounded unto death. The flash shone full in the scientist's face, blinding him. Fingers tugged awkwardly at his cords, a knife edge was dragged across them, slicing skin as well as hemp.

Jugra Singh sank to the floor. The flash thumped beside him and went out. Brill groped for him, found his shoulder. The cloth was soaked with what Brill knew was blood.

"You spoke truth, *sahib*," the Sikh whispered. "How the call came in the likeness of your voice, I do not know. But I know, now, what slew Reynolds, *sahib*. After all these years—but they never forget, though the broad sea lies between. Beware! The fiend may return. The gold—the gold was cursed—I told Reynolds, *sahib*—had he heeded me, he—"

A sudden welling of blood drowned the laboring voice. Under Brill's hand the great body stiffened and twisted in a brief convulsion, then went limp.

Groping on the floor, the scientist failed to find the flashlight. He groped along the wall, found the switch and flooded the cottage with light.

Turning back into the room, a stifled cry escaped his lips.

Jugra Singh lay slumped near the bed; huddled in a corner was Yut Wuen, his yellow hands, palms upturned, limp on the floor at his sides; Ali sprawled face down in the middle of the room. All three were dead. Throats, breasts and bellies were slashed to ribbons; their garments were in strips, and among the rags hung bloody tatters of flesh. Yut Wuen had been disemboweled, and the gaping wounds of the others were like those of sheep after a mountain lion has ranged through the fold.

A blackjack still stuck in Yut Wuen's belt. Ali's dead hand clutched a knife, but it was unstained. Death had struck them before they could use their weapons. But on the floor near Jugra Singh lay a great curved dagger, and it was red to the hilt. Bloody stains led across the floor and up over the window sill. Brill found the flash, snapped it on, and leaned out the window, playing the white beam on the ground outside. Dark, irregular splotches showed, leading off toward the dense woods.

With the flash in one hand and the Sikh's knife in the other, Brill followed those stains. At the edge of the trees he came upon a track, and the short hairs lifted on his scalp. A foot, planted in a pool of blood, had limned its imprint in crimson on the hard loam. And the foot, bare and splay, was that of a human.

That print upset vague theories of a feline or anthropoid killer, stirred nebulous thoughts at the back of his mind—dim and awful race memories of semi-human ghouls, of werewolves who walked like men and slew like beasts.

A low groan brought him to a halt, his flesh crawling. Under the black trees in the silence, that sound was pregnant with grisly probabilities. Gripping the knife firmly, he flashed the beam ahead of him. The thin light wavered, then focused on a black heap that was not part of the forest.

Brill bent over the figure and stood transfixed, transported back across the years and across the world to another wilder, grimmer woodland.

It was a naked black man that lay at his feet, his glassy eyes reflecting the waning light. His legs were short, bowed and gnarled, his arms long, his shoulders abnormally broad, his shaven head set plump between them without visible neck. That head was hideously malformed; the forehead projected almost into a peek, while the back of the skull was unnaturally flattened. White paint banded face, shoulders and breast. But it was at the creature's fingers which Brill looked longest. At first glance they seemed monstrously deformed. Then he saw that those hands were furnished with long curving steel hooks, sharp-pointed, and keen-edged on the concave side. To each finger one of these barbarous weapons was made fast, and those fingers, like the hooks clotted and smeared with blood, twitched exactly as the talons of a leopard twitch.

A light step brought him round. His dimming light played on a tall figure, and Brill mumbled: "John Galt!" in no great surprise. He was so numbed by bewilderment that the strangeness of the man's presence did not occur to him.

"What in God's name is this?" demanded the tall explorer, taking the light from Brill's hand and directing it on the mangled shape. "What in Heaven's name is that?"

"A black nightmare from Africa!" Brill found his tongue at last, and speech came in a rush. "An Egbo! A leopard man! I learned of them when I was on the West Coast. He belongs to a native cult which worships the leopard. They take a male infant and subject his head to pressure, to make it deformed; and he is brought up to believe that the spirit of a leopard inhabits his body. He does the bidding of the cult's head, which mainly consists of executing the enemies of the cult. He is, in effect, a human leopard!"

"What's he doing here?" demanded Galt, in seeming incredulity.

"God knows. But he must have been the thing that killed Reynolds. He killed Reynolds' three servants tonight—would have killed me, too, I suppose, but Jugra Singh wounded him, and he evidently dragged himself away like a wild beast to die in the jungle—"

Galt seemed curiously uninterested in Brill's stammering narrative.

"Sure he's dead?" he muttered, bending closer to flash the light into the hideous face. The illumination was dim; the battery was swiftly burning out.

As Brill was about to speak, the painted face was briefly convulsed. The glazed eyes gleamed as with a last surge of life. A clawed hand stirred, lifted feebly up toward Galt. A few gutturals seeped through the blubbery lips; the fingers writhed weakly, slipped from the iron talons, which the black man lifted, as if trying to hand them to Galt. Then he shuddered, sank back and lay still. He had been stabbed under the heart, and only a beast-like vitality had carried him so far.

Galt straightened and faced Brill, turning the light on him. A beat of silence cut between them, in which the atmosphere was electric with tension.

"You understand the Ekoi dialect?" It was more an assertion than a question.

Brill's heart was pounding, a new bewilderment vying with a rising wrath. "Yes," he answered shortly.

"What did that fool say?" softly asked Galt.

Brill set his teeth and stubbornly took the plunge reason cried out against. "He said," he replied between his teeth, "'Master, take my tools to the tribe, and tell them of our vengeance; they will give you what I promised you.'"

Even as he ground out the words, his powerful body crouched, his nerves taut for the grapple. But before he could move, the black muzzle of an automatic trained on his belly.

"Too bad you had to understand that death-bed confession, Brill," said Galt, coolly. "I don't want to kill you. I've kept blood off *my* hands so far through this affair. Listen, you're a poor man, like most scientists—how'd you consider cutting in on a fortune? Wouldn't that be preferable to getting a slug through your guts and being planted alongside those yellow-bellied stiffs down in Reynolds' shack for them to get the blame?"

"No man wants to die," answered Brill, his gaze fixed on the light in Galt's hand—the glow which was rapidly turning redder and dimmer.

"Good!" snapped Galt. "I'll give you the low down. Reynolds got his money in the Kameroons—stole gold from the Ekoi, which they had stored in the ju-ju hut; he killed a priest of the Egbo cult in getting away. Jugra Singh was with him. But they didn't get all the gold. And after that the Ekoi took good care to guard it so nobody could steal what was left.

"I knew this fellow, Guja, when I was in Africa. I was after the Ekoi gold then, but I never had a chance to locate it. I met Guja a few months ago, again. He'd been exiled from his tribe for some crime, had wandered to the Coast and been picked up with some more natives who were brought to America for exhibition in the World's Fair.

"Guja was mad to get back to his people, and he spilled the whole story of the gold. Told me that if he could kill Reynolds, his tribe would forgive him. He knew that Reynolds was somewhere in America, but he was helpless as a child to find him. I offered to arrange his meeting with the gold-thief, if Guja would agree to give me some of the gold his tribe hoarded.

"He swore by the skull of the great leopard. I brought him secretly into these hills, and hid him up yonder in a shack the existence of which nobody suspects. It took me a wretched time to teach him just what he was to do—he'd no more brains than an ape. Night after night I went through the thing with him, until he learned the procedure: to watch in the hills until he saw a light flash in Reynolds' shack. Then steal down there, jerk the switch—and kill. These leopard men can see like cats at night.

"I called Reynolds up myself; it wasn't hard to imitate your voice. I used to do impersonations in vaudeville. While Guja was tearing the life out of Reynolds, I was dining at a well-known night club, in full sight of all.

"I came here tonight to smuggle him out of the country. But his blood-lust must have betrayed him. When he saw the light flash on in the cottage again, it must have started a train of associations that led him once more to the cottage, to kill whoever he found there. I saw the tag-end of the business—saw him stagger away from the shack, and then you follow him.

"Now then, I've shot the works. Nobody knows I'm mixed up in this business, but you. Will you keep your mouth shut and take a share of the Ekoi gold?"

The glow went out. In the sudden darkness, Brill, his pent-up feelings exploding at last, yelled: "Damn you, no! You murdering dog!" and sprang aside. The pistol cracked, an orange jet sliced the darkness, and the bullet fanned Brill's ear as he threw the heavy knife blindly. He heard it rattle futilely through the bushes, and stood frozen with the realization that he had lost his desperate gamble.

But even as he braced himself against the tearing impact of the bullet he expected, a sudden beam drilled the blackness, illuminating the convulsed features of John Galt.

"Don't move, Galt; I've got the drop on you."

It was the voice of Buckley. With a snarl, Galt took as desperate a chance as Brill had taken. He wheeled toward the source of the light, snapping down his automatic. But even as he did so, the detective's .45 crashed, and outlined against the brief glare, Galt swayed and fell like a tall tree struck by lightning.

"Dead?" asked the scientist, mechanically.

"Bullet tore through his forearm and smashed his shoulder," grunted Buckley. "Just knocked out temporarily. He'll live to decorate the gallows."

"You—you heard—?" Brill stuttered.

"Everything. I was just coming around the bend of the lake shore and saw a light in Reynolds' cottage, then your flash bobbing among the trees. I came sneaking through the bushes just in time to hear you give your translation of the nigger's dying words. I've been prowling around this lake all night."

"You suspected Galt all the time?"

The detective grinned wryly.

"I ought to say yes, and establish myself as a super sleuth. But the fact is, I suspected *you* all the time. That's why I came up here tonight—trying to figure out your connection with the murder. That alibi of yours was so iron-clad it looked phony to me. I had a sneaking suspicion that I'd bumped into a master-mind trying to put over the 'perfect crime.' I apologize! I've been reading too many detective stories lately!"

FANGS OF GOLD

This is the only trail into the swamp, mister." Steve Harrison's guide pointed a long finger down the narrow path which wound in and out among the live-oaks and cypresses. Harrison shrugged his massive shoulders. The surroundings were not inviting, with the long shadows of the late afternoon sun reaching dusky fingers into the dim recesses among the moss-hung trees.

"You ought to wait till mornin'," opined the guide, a tall lanky man in cowhide boots and sagging overall. "It's gittin' late, and we don't want to git catched in the swamp after night."

"I can't wait, Rogers," answered the detective. "The man I'm after might get clean away by morning."

"He'll have to come out by this path," answered Rogers as they swung along. "Ain't no other way in or out. If he tries to push through to high ground on the other side, he'll shore fall into a bottomless bog, or git et by a gator. There's lots of them. I reckon he ain't much used to swamps?"

"I don't suppose he ever saw one before. He's city-bred."

"Then he won't das't leave the beaten path," confidently predicted Rogers.

"On the other hand, he might, not realizing the danger," grunted Harrison.

"What'd you say he done?" pursued Rogers, directing a jet of tobacco juice at a beetle crawling through the dark loam.

"Knocked an old Chinaman in the head with a meat-cleaver and stole his life-time savings—ten thousand dollars, in bills of a thousand each. The old man left a little granddaughter who'll be penniless if this money isn't recovered. That's one reason I want to get this rat before he loses himself in a bog. I want to recover that money, for the kid."

"And you figure the Chinaman seen goin' down this path a few days ago was him?"

"Couldn't be anybody else," snapped Harrison. "We've hounded him half way across the continent, cut him off from the borders and the ports. We were closing in on him when he slipped through, somehow. This was about the only place left for him to hide. I've chased him too far to delay now. If he drowns in the swamp, we'll probably never find him, and the money will be lost, too. The man he murdered was a fine, honest old Chinaman. This fellow, Woon Shang, is bad all the way through."

"He'll run into some bad folks down here," ruminated Rogers. "Nothin' but niggers live in these swamplands. They ain't regular darkies like them that live outside. These came here fifty or sixty years back—refugees from Haiti, or somewhere. You know we ain't far from the coast. They're yeller-skinned, and don't hardly ever come out of the swamp. They keep to theirselves, and they don't like strangers. *What's that?*"

They were just rounding a bend in the path, and something lay on the ground ahead of them—something black, and dabbled with red, that groaned and moved feebly.

"It's a nigger!" exclaimed Rogers. "He's been knifed."

It took no expert to deduce that. They bent over him and Rogers voiced profane recognition. "Why, I know this feller! He ain't no swamp rat. He's Joe Corley, that razored up another nigger at a dance last month and lit out. Bet he's been hidin' in the swamp ever since. Joe! Joe Corley!"

The wounded man groaned and rolled up his glassy eyes; his skin was ashy with the nearness of approaching death.

"Who stabbed you, Joe?" demanded Rogers.

"De Swamp Cat!" The gasp was scarcely audible. Rogers swore and looked fearfully about him, as if expecting something to spring on them from the trees.

"I wuz tryin' to git outside," muttered the Negro.

"What for?" demanded Rogers. "Didn't you know you'd git jailed if they catched you?"

"Ruther go to de jail-house dan git mixed up—in de devilment— dey's cookin' up—in de swamp." The voice sank lower as speech grew more difficult.

"What you mean, Joe?" uneasily demanded Rogers.

"Voodoo niggers," muttered Corley disjointedly. "Took dat Chinaman 'stead uh me—didn't want me to git away, though—then John Bartholomew—uuuugh!"

A trickle of blood started from the corner of his thick lips, he stiffened in brief convulsion and then lay still.

"He's dead!" whispered Rogers, staring down the swamp path with dilated eyes.

"He spoke of a Chinaman," said Harrison. "That clinches it that we're on the right trail. Have to leave him here for the time being. Nothing we can do for him now. Let's get going."

"You aim to go on, after this?" exclaimed Rogers.

"Why not?"

"Mr. Harrison," said Rogers solemnly, "you offered me a good wage to guide you into this here swamp. But I'm tellin' you fair there ain't enough money to make me go in there now, with night comin' on."

"But why?" protested Harrison. Just because this man got into a fight with one of his own kind—"

"It's more 'n just that," declared Rogers decisively. "This nigger was tryin' to git out of the swamp when they got him. He knowed he'd git jailed on the outside, but he was goin' anyway; that means somethin' had scared the livin' daylights out of him. You heard him say it was the Swamp Cat that got him?"

"Well?"

"Well, the Swamp Cat is a crazy nigger that lives in the swamp. It's been so long since any white folks claimed they seen him, I'd begun to believe he was just a myth the 'outside' niggers told to scare people away from the swamp. But this shows he ain't. He killed Joe Corley. He'll kill us if he catches us in the dark. Why, by golly, he may be watchin' us right now!" This thought so disturbed Rogers that he drew a big six-shooter with an enormous length of barrel, and peered about, masticating his quid with a rapidity that showed his mental perturbation.

"Who's the other follow he named, John Bartholomew?" inquired Harrison.

"Don't know. Never heard of him. Come on, let's shove out of here. We'll git some boys and come back after Joe's body."

"I'm going on," growled Harrison, rising and dusting his hands.

Rogers stared. "Man, you're plumb crazy! You'll git lost—"

"Not if I keep to the path."

"Well, then, the Swamp Cat'll git you, or them gators will—"

"I'll take my chance," answered Harrison brusquely. "Woon Shang's somewhere in this swamp. If he manages to get out before I get my hands on him, he may get clean away. I'm going after him."

"But if you'll wait we'll raise a posse and go after him first thing in the mornin'," urged Rogers.

Harrison did not attempt to explain to the man his almost obsessional preference for working alone. With no further comment he turned and strode off down the narrow path. Rogers yelled after him: "You're crazy as Hell! If you git as far as Celia Pompoloi's hut, you better stay there tonight! She's the big boss of them niggers. It's the first cabin you come to. I'm goin' back to town and git a posse, and to-morrow mornin' we'll—" The words became unintelligible among the dense growth as Harrison rounded a turn that shut off the sight of the other man.

As the detective strode along he saw that blood was smeared on the rotting leaves, and there were marks as if something heavy had been dragged over the trail. Joe Corley had obviously crawled for some distance after being attacked. Harrison visualized him dragging himself along on his belly like a crippled snake. The man must have had intense vitality to have gotten so far with a mortal wound in his back. And his fear must have been desperate to so drive him.

Harrison could no longer see the sun, but he knew it was hanging low. The shadows were gathering, and he was plunging deeper and deeper into the swamp. He began to glimpse patches of scummy ooze among the trees, and the path grew more tortuous as it wound to avoid these slimy puddles. Harrison plunged on without pausing. The dense growth might lend concealment to a desperate fugitive, but it was not in the woods, but among the scattered cabins of the swamp dwellers that he expected to find the man he hunted. The city-bred Chinaman, fearful of solitude and unable to fend for himself, would seek the company of men, even of black men.

The detective wheeled suddenly. About him, in the dusk, the swamp was waking. Insects lifted strident voices, wings of bats or owls beat the air, and bullfrogs boomed from the lily pads. But he had heard a sound that was not of these things. It was a stealthy movement among the trees that marched in solid ranks beside the trail. Harrison drew his .45 and waited. Nothing happened. But in primitive solitudes a man's instincts are whetted. The detective felt that he was being watched by unseen eyes; he could almost sense the intensity of their glare. Was it the Chinaman, after all?

A bush beside the trail moved, without a wind to stir it. Harrison sprang through the curtain of creeper-hung cypresses, gun ready, snarling a command. His feet sank in slimy ooze, he stumbled in rotting vegetation and felt the dangling strands of moss slap against his face. There was nothing behind the bush, but he could have sworn that he saw a shadowy form move and vanish among the trees a short distance away. As he hesitated, he glanced down and saw a distinct mark in the loam. He bent closer; it was the print of a great, bare, splay foot. Moisture was oozing into the depression. A man *had* been standing behind that bush.

With a shrug Harrison stepped back into the trail. That was not the footprint of Woon Shang, and the detective was not looking for anybody else. It was natural that one of the swamp dwellers would spy on a stranger. The detective sent a hail into the gathering darkness, to assure the unseen watcher of his friendly intentions. There was no reply. Harrison turned and strode on down the trail, not feeling entirely at ease, as he heard, from time to time, a faint snapping of twigs and other sounds that seemed to indicate someone moving along a course paralleling the path. It was not soothing to know that he was being followed by some unseen and possibly hostile being.

It was so dark now that he kept the path more by feel than by sight. About him sounded weird cries of strange birds or animals, and from time to time a deep grunting reverberation that puzzled him until he recognized it as the bellow of a bull alligator. He wondered if the scaly brutes ever crawled up on the trail, and how the fellow that was shadowing him out there in the darkness managed to avoid them. With the thought another twig snapped, much closer to the trail than before. Harrison swore softly, trying to peer into the Stygian gloom under the moss-festooned branches. The fellow was closing in on him with the growing darkness.

There was a sinister implication about the thing that made Harrison's flesh creep a bit. This reptile-haunted swamp-trail was no place for a fight with an insane Negro—for it seemed probable that the unknown stalker was the killer of Joe Corley. Harrison was meditating on the matter when a light glimmered through the trees ahead of him. Quickening his steps he came abruptly out of the darkness into a grey twilight.

He had reached an expanse of solid ground, where the thinning trees let in the last grey light of the outer dusk. They made a black wall with waving fringes all about a small clearing, and through their boles, on one side, Harrison caught a glimmer of inky water. In the clearing stood a cabin of rough-hewn logs, and through a tiny window shone the light of an oil lamp.

As Harrison emerged from among the growth he glanced back, but saw no movement among the ferns, heard no sound of pursuit. The path, dimly marked on the higher ground, ran past the cabin and vanished in the further gloom. This cabin must be the abode of that Celia Pompoloi Rogers had mentioned. Harrison strode to the sagging stoop and rapped on the handmade door.

Inside there was movement, and the door swung open. Harrison was not prepared for the figure that confronted him. He had expected to see a bare-footed slattern; instead he saw a tall, rangily powerful man, neatly dressed, whose regular features and light skin portrayed his mixed blood.

"Good evening, sir." The accent hinted of education above the average.

"Name's Harrison," said the detective abruptly, displaying his badge. "I'm after a crook that ran in here—a Chinese murderer, named Woon Shang. Know anything about him?"

"Yes, sir," the man replied promptly. "That man went past my cabin three days ago."

"Where is he now?" demanded Harrison.

The other spread his hands in a curiously Latin gesture.

"I can not say. I have little intercourse with the other people who live in the swamp, but it is my belief that he is hiding among them somewhere. I have not seen him pass my cabin going back up the path."

"Can you guide me to these other cabins?"

"Gladly, sir; by daylight."

"I'd like to go tonight," growled Harrison.

"That's impossible, sir," the other protested. "It would be most dangerous. You ran a great risk in coming this far alone. The other cabins are further back in the swamp. We do not leave our huts at night; there are many things in the swamp which are dangerous to human beings."

"The Swamp Cat, for instance?" grunted Harrison.

The man cast him a quick glance of interrogation.

"He killed a colored man named Joe Corley a few hours ago," said the detective. "I found Corley on the trail. And if I'm not mistaken, that same lunatic has been following me for the past half hour."

The mulatto evinced considerable disquiet and glanced across the clearing into the shadows.

"Come in," he urged. "If the Swamp Cat is prowling tonight, no man is safe out of door. Come in and spend the night with me, and at dawn I will guide you to all the cabins in the swamp."

Harrison saw no better plan. After all, it was absurd to go blundering about in the night, in an unknown marsh. He realized that he had made a mistake in coming in by himself, in the dusk; but working alone had become a habit with him, and he was tinged with a strong leaven of recklessness. Following a tip he had arrived at the little town on the edge of the swamplands in the mid-afternoon, and plunged on into the woods without hesitation. Now he doubted the wisdom of the move.

"Is this Celia Pompoloi's cabin?" he asked.

"It was," the mulatto replied. "She has been dead for three weeks. I live here alone. My name is John Bartholomew."

Harrison's head snapped up and he eyed the other with new interest. John Bartholomew; Joe Corley had muttered that name just before he died.

"Did you know Joe Corley?" he demanded.

"Slightly; he came into the swamp to hide from the law. He was a rather low grade sort of human, though naturally I am sorry to hear of his death."

"What's a man of your intelligence and education doing in this jungle?" the detective asked bluntly.

Bartholomew smiled rather wryly. "We can not always choose our environments, Mr. Harrison. The waste places of the world provide retreat for others than criminals. Some come to the swamps like your Chinaman, fleeing from the law. Others come to forget bitter disappointments forced upon them by circumstances."

Harrison glanced about the cabin while Bartholomew was putting a stout bar in place across the door. It had but two rooms, one behind the other, connected by a strongly built door. The slab floor was clean, the room scantily furnished; a table, benches, a bunk built against the wall, all hand-made. There was a fireplace, over which hung primitive cooking utensils, and a cloth covered cupboard.

"Would you like some fried bacon and corn pone?" asked Bartholomew. "Or perhaps a cup of coffee? I do not have much to offer you, but—"

"No, thanks, I ate a big meal just before I started into the swamp.

Just tell me something about these people."

"As I said, I have little intercourse with them," answered Bartholomew. "They are clannish and suspicious, and keep much to themselves. They are not like other colored people. Their fathers came here from Haiti, following one of the bloody revolutions which have cursed that unfortunate island in the past. They have curious customs. Have you heard of the worship of Voodoo?"

Harrison nodded.

"These people are Voodooists. I know that they have mysterious conclaves back in the swamps. I have heard drums booming in the night, and seen the glow of fires through the trees. I have sometimes felt a little uneasy for my safety at such times. Such people are capable of bloody extremes, when their primitive natures are maddened by the bestial rites of the Voodoo."

"Why don't the whites come in here and stop it?" demanded Harrison.

"They know nothing about it. No one ever comes here unless he is a fugitive from the law. The swamp people carry on their worship without interference.

"Celia Pompoloi, who once occupied this very hut, was a woman of considerable intelligence and some education; she was the one swamp dweller who ever went 'outside,' as they call the outer world, and attended school. Yet, to my actual knowledge, she was the priestess of the cult and presided over their rituals. It is my belief that she met her fate at last during one of those saturnalias. Her body was found in the marshes, so badly mangled by the alligators that it was recognizable only by her garments."

"What about the Swamp Cat?" asked Harrison.

"A maniac, living like a wild beast in the marshes, only sporadically violent; but at those times a thing of horror."

"Would be kill the Chinaman if he had a chance?"

"He would kill anyone when his fit is on him. You said the Chinaman was a murderer?"

"Murderer and thief," grunted Harrison. "Stole ten grand from the man he killed."

Bartholomew looked up as with renewed interest, started to speak, then evidently changed his mind.

Harrison rose, yawning. "Think I'll hit the hay," he announced.

Bartholomew took up the lamp and led his guest into the back room, which was of the same size as the other, but whose furnishings consisted only of a bunk and a bench.

"I have but the one lamp, sir," said Bartholomew. "I shall leave it with you."

"Don't bother," grunted Harrison, having a secret distrust of oil lamps, resultant from experiencing an explosion of one in his boyhood. "I'm like a cat in the dark. I don't need it."

With many apologies for the rough accommodations and wishes for a good night's sleep, Bartholomew bowed himself out, and the door closed. Harrison, through force of habit, studied the room. A little starlight came in through the one small window, which he noticed was furnished with heavy wooden bars. There was no door other than the one by which he had entered. He lay down on the bunk fully dressed, without even removing his shoes, and pondered rather glumly. He was beset by fears that Woon Shang might escape him, after all. Suppose the Chinaman slipped out by the way he had come in? True, local officers were watching at the edge of the swampland, but Woon Shang might avoid them in the night. And what if there *was* another way out, known only to the swamp people? And if Bartholomew was as little acquainted with his neighbors as he said, what assurance was there that the mulatto would be able to guide him to the

Chinaman's hiding place? These and other doubts assailed him while he lay and listened to the soft sounds of his host's retiring, and saw the thin line of light under the door vanish as the lamp was blown out. At last Harrison consigned his doubts to the devil, and fell asleep.

CHAPTER II
Murder Tracks

It was a noise at the windows, a stealthy twisting and wrenching at the bars, that awakened him. He woke quickly, with all his facilities alert, as was his habit. Something bulked in the window, something dark and round, with gleaming spots in it. He realized with a start that it was a human head he saw, with the faint starlight shining on rolling eyes and bared teeth. Without shifting his body, the detective stealthily reached for his gun; lying as he was in the darkness of the bunk, the man watching him could scarcely have seen the movement. But the head vanished, as if warned by some instinct.

Harrison sat up on his bunk, scowling, resisting the natural impulse to rush to the window and look out. That might be exactly what the man outside was wanting. There was something deadly about this business; the fellow had evidently been trying to get in. Was it the same creature that had followed him through the swamp? A sudden thought struck him. What was more likely than that the Chinaman had set a man to watch for a possible pursuer? Harrison cursed himself for not having thought of it before.

He struck a match, cupped it in his hand, and looked at his watch. It was scarcely ten o'clock. The night was still young. He scowled abstractedly at the rough wall behind the bunk, minutely illuminated in the flare of the match, and suddenly his breath hissed between his teeth. The match burned down to his fingers and went out. He struck another and leaned to the wall. Thrust in a chink between the logs was a knife, and its wicked curved blade was grimly smeared and clotted. The implication sent a shiver down Harrison's spine. The blood might be that of an animal—but who would butcher a calf or a hog in that room? Why had not the blade been cleansed? It was as if it had been hastily concealed, after striking a murderous blow.

He took it down and looked at it closely. The blood was dried and blackened as if at least many hours had elapsed since it had been let. The weapon was no ordinary butcher knife—Harrison stiffened. *It was a Chinese dagger.* The match went out and Harrison did what the average man would have done. He leaned over the edge of the bunk, the only thing in the room that would conceal an object of any size, and lifted the cloth that hung to the floor. He did not actually expect to find the corpse of Woon Shang beneath it. He merely acted through instinct. Nor did he find a corpse. His hand, groping in the dark, encountered only the uneven floor and rough logs; then his fingers felt something else—something at once compact and yielding, wedged between the logs as the knife had been.

He drew it forth; it felt like a flat package of crisp paper, bound with oiled silk. Cupping a match in his hand, he tore it open. Ten worn bills met his gaze; on each bill was the numerals of $1,000. He crushed the match out and sat in the dark, mental pictures tumbling rapidly across his consciousness.

So John Bartholomew had lied. Doubtless he had taken in the Chinaman as he had taken in Harrison. The detective visualized a dim form bending in the darkness above a sleeping figure in that same bunk—a murderous stroke with the victim's own knife.

He growled inarticulately, with the chagrin of the cheated manhunter, certain that Woon Shang's body was rotting in some slimy marsh. At least he had the money. Careless of Bartholomew to hide it there. But was it? It was only by an accidental chain of circumstances that he had found it—

He stiffened again. Under the door he saw a thin pencil of light. Had Bartholomew not yet gone to bed? But he remembered the blowing out of the lamp. Harrison rose and glided noiselessly to the thick door. When he reached it he heard a low mumble of voices in the outer room. The speakers moved nearer, stood directly before the door. He strained his ears and recognized the crisp accents of John Bartholomew. "Don't bungle the job," the mulatto was muttering. "Get him before he has a chance to use his gun. He doesn't suspect anything. I just remember that I left the Chinaman's knife in the crack over the bunk. But the detective will never see it, in the dark. He had to come butting in here, this particular night. We can't let him see what he'd see if he lived through this night."

"We do de job quick and clean, mastah," murmured another voice, with a guttural accent different from any Harrison had ever heard, and impossible to reproduce.

"Alright; we haven't anything to fear from Joe Corley. The Swamp Cat carried out my instructions."

"Dat Swamp Cat prowlin' 'round outside right now," muttered another man. "Ah don't like him. Why can't he do dis job?"

'He obeys my orders; but he can't be trusted too far. But we can't stand here talking like this. The detective will wake up and get suspicious. Throw open that door and rush him. Knife him in his bunk—"

Harrison always believed that the best defense was a strong offensive. There was but one way out of this jam. He took it without hesitation. He hurled a massive shoulder against the door, knocking it open, and sprang into the outer room, gun leveled, and barked: "Hands up, damn you!"

There were five men in that room; Bartholomew, holding the

lamp and shading it with his left hand, and four others, four lean, rangy giants in nondescript garments, with yellow, sinister features. Each man of the four had a knife in his hand.

They recoiled with yells of dismay as Harrison crashed upon them. Automatically their hands went up and their knives clattered on the floor. For an instant the white man was complete master of the situation, Bartholomew turning ashy as he stared, the lamp shaking in his hands.

"Back up against that wall!" snapped Harrison.

They obeyed dumbly, rendered incapable of action by the shock of surprise. Harrison knew that it was John Bartholomew, more than these hulking butchers, that he had to fear.

"Set that lamp on the table," he snapped. "Line up there with them—*ha!*"

Bartholomew had stooped to lower the lamp to the table—then quick as a cat he threw it crashing to the floor, ducking behind the table with the same motion. Harrison's gun crashed almost simultaneously, but even in the bedlam darkness that followed, the detective knew he had missed. Whirling, he leaped through the outer door. Inside the dark cabin he would have no chance against the knives for which the Negroes were already groping on the floor, mouthing like rabid dogs. As Harrison raced across the clearing he heard Bartholomew's furious voice yelling commands. The white man did not take the obvious route, the beaten trail. He rounded the cabin and darted toward the trees on the other side. He had no intention of fleeing until he was run down from behind. He was seeking a place where he could turn at bay and shoot it out with a little advantage on his side. The moon was just coming up above the trees, emphasizing, rather than illuminating the shadows.

He heard the Negroes clamoring out of the cabin and casting

about, momentarily at a loss. He reached the shadows before they rounded the hut, and glancing back through the bushes, saw them running about the clearing like hunting dogs seek a spoor, howling in primitive blood-lust and disappointment. The growing moonlight glittered on the long knives in their hands.

He drew back further among the trees, finding the ground more solid underfoot than he had expected. Then he came suddenly upon the marshy edge of a stretch of black water. Something grunted and thrashed amidst it, and two green lamps burned suddenly like jewels on the inky water. He recoiled, well knowing what those twin lights were. And as he did so, he bumped full into something that locked fierce arms like an ape about him.

Harrison ducked and heaved, bowing his powerful back like a great cat, and his assailant tumbled over his head and thumped on the ground, still clutching the detective's coat with the grip of a vise. Harrison lunged backward, ripping the garment down the back, wrenching his arms from the sleeves, in his frenzy to free himself.

The man leaped to his feet on the edge of the pool, snarling like a wild beast. Harrison saw a gaunt half naked black man with wild strands of hair caked with mud hanging over a contorted mask of a face, the thick loose lips drooling foam. This, indeed, he knew, was the dread Swamp Cat.

Still grasping Harrison's torn coat brainlessly in his left hand, his right swept up with a sheen of sharp steel, and even as he sensed the madman's intention, the detective ducked and fired from the hip. The thrown knife hummed by his ear, and with the crash of the shot the Swamp Cat swayed and pitched backward into the black pool. There was a threshing rush, the waters stormed foamily, there was a glimpse of a blunted, reptilian snout, and the trailing body vanished with it.

Harrison stepped back, sickened, and heard behind him the shouting progress of men through the bushes. His hunters had heard the shot. He drew back into the shadows among a cluster of gum trees, and waited, gun in hand. An instant later they rushed out upon the bank of the pool, John Bartholomew and his dusky knife-fighters.

They ranged the bank, gaping, and then Bartholomew laughed and pointed to a blood-stained piece of cloth that floated soggily on the foam-flecked waters.

"The fool's coat! He must have run right into the pool, and the 'gator's got him! I can see them tearing at something, over there among the reeds. Hear those bones crack?" Bartholomew's laugh was fiendish to hear.

"Well," said the mulatto, "we don't have to worry about him. If they send anybody in after him, we'll just tell them the truth: that he fell into the water and got grabbed by the gators, just like Celia Pompoloi."

"She wuz a awful sight when us foun' huh body," muttered one of the swamp Negroes.

"We'll never find that much of him," prophesied Bartholomew.

"Did he say what de Chinaman done?" asked another of the men.

"Just what the Chinaman said; that he'd murdered a man."

"Wish he'd uh robbed uh bank," murmured the swamp dweller plaintively. "Wish he'd uh brung uh lot uh money in wid him."

"Well, he didn't," snapped Bartholomew. "You saw me search him. Now get back to the others and help them watch him. These Chinese are slippery customers, and we can't take any chances with him. More white men may come looking for him tomorrow, but if they do, they're welcome to all of him they can find!" He laughed with sinister meaning, and then added abruptly: "Hurry and get out of here. I want to be alone. There are spirits to be communed with before the hour arrives, and dread rites that I must perform alone. Go!"

The others bent their heads in a curious gesture of subservience, and trooped away, in the direction of the clearing. He followed leisurely.

Harrison glared after them, turning what he had heard over in his mind. Some of it was gibberish, but certain things were clear. For one thing, the Chinaman was obviously alive, and imprisoned somewhere. Bartholomew had lied about his own relations with the swamp people; one of them he certainly was not; but he was just as certainly a leader among them. Yet he had lied to them about the Chinaman's money. Harrison remembered the mulatto's expression when he had mentioned it to him. The detective believed that Bartholomew had never seen the money; that Woon Shang, suspicious, had hidden it himself before he was attacked.

Harrison rose and stole after the retreating Negroes. As long as they believed him dead, he could conduct his investigations without being harried by pursuit. His shirt was of dark material and did not show in the darkness, and the big detective was trained in stealth by adventures in the haunted dives of Oriental quarters where unseen eyes always watched and ears were forever alert.

When he came to the edge of the trees, he saw the four giants trooping down the trail that led deeper into the swamp. They walked in single file, their heads bent forward, stooping from the waist like apes. Bartholomew was just going into the cabin. Harrison started to follow the disappearing forms, then hesitated. Bartholomew was in his power. He could steal up on the cabin, throw his gun on the mulatto and make him tell where Woon Shang was imprisoned—maybe. Harrison knew the invincible stubbornness of the breed. Even as he ruminated, Bartholomew came out of the cabin and stood peering about with a strange furtiveness. He held a heavy whip in his hand. Presently he glided across the clearing toward the quarter where the detective crouched. He passed within a few yards of Harrison's covert, and the moonlight illumined his features. Harrison was astounded at the change in his face, at the sinister vitality and evil strength reflected there.

Harrison altered his plans and stole after him, wishing to know on what errand the man went with such secrecy. It was not difficult. Bartholomew looked neither back nor sidewise, but wound a tortuous way among inky pools and clusters of rotting vegetation that looked poisonous, even in the moonlight. Presently the detective crouched low; ahead of the mulatto there was a tiny hut, almost hidden among the trees which trailed Spanish moss over it like a grey veil. Bartholomew looked carefully about him, then drew forth a key and manipulated a large padlock on the door. Harrison was convinced that he had been led to the prison of Woon Shang.

Bartholomew disappeared inside, closing the door. A light gleamed through the chinks of the logs. Then came a mumble of voices, too indistinct for Harrison to tell anything about them; that was followed by the sharp, unmistakable crack of a whip on bare flesh, and a shrill cry of pain. Enlightenment came to Harrison. Bartholomew had come secretly to his prisoner, to torture the Chinaman—and for what reason but to make him divulge the hiding place of the money, of which Harrison had spoken? Obviously Bartholomew had no intentions of sharing that money with his mates.

Harrison began to work his way stealthily toward the cabin, fully intending to burst in and put a stop to that lashing. He would cheerfully have shot down Woon Shang himself, had the occasion arisen, but he had a white man's abhorrence of torture. But before he reached the hut, the sounds ceased, the light went out and Bartholomew emerged, wiping the perspiration of exertion from his brow. He locked the door, thrust the key in his pocket, and turned away through the trees, trailing his whip in his hand. Harrison, crouching in the shadows, let him go. It was Woon Shang he was after. Bartholomew could be dealt with later.

When the mulatto had disappeared, Harrison rose and strode to the door of the hut. The absence of guards was rather puzzling, after the conversation he had overheard, but be wasted no time on conjecture. The door was secured by a chain made fast to a big hasp driven deep into a log. He thrust his gun barrel through this hasp, and using it as a lever, pried out the hasp with no great difficulty.

Pulling open the door he peered in; it was too dark to see, but be heard somebody's breath coming in jerky hysterical sobs. He struck a match, looked—then glared. The prisoner was there, crouching on the dirt floor. But it was not Woon Shang. It was a woman.

She was a mulatto, young, and handsome in her way. She was clad only in a ragged and scanty chemise, and her hands were bound behind her. From her wrists a long strand of rawhide ran to a heavy staple in the wall. She stared wildly at Harrison, her dark eyes reflecting both hope and terror. There were tear stains on her checks.

"Who the devil are you?" demanded the detective.

"Celia Pompoloi!" Her voice was rich and musical despite its hysteria. "Oh, white man, for God's sake let me go! I can't stand it any more. I'll die; I know I will!"

"I thought you *were* dead," he grunted.

"John Bartholomew did it!" she exclaimed. "He persuaded a yellow girl from 'outside' into the swamp, and then he killed her and dressed her in my clothes, and threw her into the marsh where the alligators would chew the body till nobody could tell it wasn't me. The people found it and thought it was Celia Pompoloi. He's kept me here for three weeks and tortured me every night."

"Why?" Harrison found and lighted a candle stump stuck on the wall. Then he stooped and cut the rawhide thongs that bound her hands. She climbed to her feet, chafing her bruised and swollen wrists. In her scanty garb the brutality of the floggings she had received was quite apparent.

"He's a devil!" Her dark eyes flashed murderously; whatever her wrongs, she obviously was no meek sufferer. "He came here posing as a priest of the Great Serpent. He said he was from Haiti, the lying dog. He's from Santo Domingo, and no more priest than you are. *I* am the proper priestess of the Serpent, and the people obeyed me. That's why he put me out of the way. I'll kill him!"

"But why did he lick you?" asked Harrison.

"Because I wouldn't tell him what be wanted to know," she muttered sullenly, bending her head and twisting one bare foot behind the other ankle, school-girl fashion. She did not seem to think of refusing to answer his questions. His white skin put him beyond and outside swamp-land politics.

"He came here to steal the jewel, the heart of the Great Serpent, which we brought with us from Haiti, long ago. He is no priest. He is an impostor. He proposed that I give the Heart to him and run away from my people with him. When I refused, he tied me in this old hut where none can hear my screams; the swamp people shun it, thinking it's haunted. He said he'd keep beating me until I told him where the Heart was hidden, but I wouldn't tell him—not though he stripped all the flesh from my bones. I alone know that secret, because I am a priestess of the Serpent, and the guardian of its heart."

This was Voodoo stuff with a vengeance; her matter-of-fact manner evinced an unshaken belief in her weird cult.

"Do you know anything about the Chinaman, Woon Shang?" he demanded.

"John Bartholomew told me of him in his boastings. He came

running from the law and Bartholomew promised to hide him. Then he summoned the swamp men, and they seized the Chinaman, though he wounded one of them badly with his knife. They made a prisoner of him—"

"Why?"

Celia was in that vengeful mood in which a woman recklessly tells everything, and repeats things she would not otherwise mention.

"Bartholomew came saying he was a priest of old time. That's how he caught the fancy of the people. He promised them an *old* sacrifice, of which there has not been one for thirty years. We have offered the white cock and the red cock to the Great Serpent. But Bartholomew promised them the *goat-without-horns*. He did that to get the Heart into his hands, for only then is it taken from its secret hiding place. He thought to get it into his hands and run away before the sacrifice was made. But when I refused to aid him, it upset his plans. Now he can not get the Heart, but he must go through with the sacrifice anyway. The people are becoming impatient. If he fails them, they will kill him.

"He first chose the 'outside' black man, Joe Corley, who was hiding in the swamp, for the sacrifice; but when the Chinaman came, Bartholomew decided be would make a better offering. Bartholomew told me tonight that the Chinaman had money, and he was going to make him tell where he hid it, so be would have the money, and the Heart, too, when I finally gave in and told him—"

"Wait a minute," interposed Harrison. "Let me get this straight. What is it that Bartholomew intends doing with Woon Shang?"

"He will offer him up to the Great Serpent," she answered, making a conventional gesture of conciliation and adoration as she spoke the dread name.

"A *human* sacrifice?"

"Yes."

"Well, I'll be damned!" he muttered. "If I hadn't been raised in the South myself, I'd never believe it. When is this sacrifice to take place?"

"Tonight!"

"Eh, what's that?" He remembered Bartholomew's cryptic instructions to his henchmen. "The devil! Where does it happen, and what time?"

"Just before dawn; far back in the swamp."

"I've got to find Woon Shang and stop it!" he exclaimed. "Where is he imprisoned?"

"At the place of the sacrifice; many men guard him. You'd never find your way there. You'd drown and get eaten by the gators. Besides, if you did get there, the people would tear you to pieces."

"You lead me there and I'll take care of the people," he snarled. "You want revenge on Bartholomew. All right; guide me there and I'll see that you get plenty. I've always worked alone," he ruminated angrily, "but the swamp country isn't River Street."

"I'll do it!" Her eyes blazed and her white teeth gleamed in a mask of passion. "I'll guide you to the place of the Altar.' We'll kill him, the yellow dog!"

"How long will it take us to get there?"

"I could go there in an hour, alone. Guiding you, it will take longer. Much longer, the way we must go. You can't travel the road I would take, alone."

"I can follow you anywhere you walk," he grunted, slightly nettled. He glanced at his watch, then extinguished the candle. "Let's get going. Take the shortest route and don't worry about me. I'll keep up."

She caught his wrist in a fierce grasp and almost jerked him out of the door, quivering with the eagerness of a hunting hound.

"Wait a minute!" A thought struck him. "If I go back to the cabin and capture Bartholomew—"

"He will not be there; he is well on his way to the Place of the Altar; better that we beat him there."

CHAPTER III
Voodoo Lair

As long as he lived Harrison remembered that race through the swamp, as he followed Celia Pompoloi along pathless ways that seemed impossible. Mire caught at his feet, and sometimes black scummy water lapped about his ankles, but Celia's swift sure feet always found solid ground where none seemed possible, or guided him over bogs that quaked menacingly beneath their weight. She sprang lightly from hummock to hummock, or slid between snaky pools of black slime where unseen monsters grunted and wallowed. Harrison floundered after her, sweating, half nauseated with the miasmic reek of the oozy slime that plastered him; but all the bulldog was roused in him, and he was ready to wade through swamps for a week if the man he hunted was at the other end of the loathsome journey. Dank misty clouds had veiled the sky, through which the moon shone fitfully, and Harrison stumbled like a blind man, depending entirely on his guide, whose dusky half-naked body was all but invisible to him at times in the darkness.

Ahead of them he began to hear a rhythmic throbbing, a barbaric pulsing that grew as they advanced. A red glow flickered through the black trees.

"The flames of the sacrifice!" gasped Celia, quickening her pace. "Hasten!"

Somewhere in his big, weary body Harrison found enough reserve energy to keep up with her. She seemed to run lightly over bogs that engulfed him to the knees. She possessed the swamp dweller's instinct for safe footing. Ahead of them Harrison saw the shine of something that was not mud, and Celia halted at the verge of a stretch of noisome water.

"The Place of the Altar is surrounded by water on all sides but one," she hissed. "We are in the very heart of the swamp, deeper than anyone ever goes except on such occasions as these. There are no cabins near. Follow me! I have a bridge none knows of except myself."

At a point where the sluggish stream narrowed to some fifty feet, a fallen tree spanned it. Celia ran out upon it, balancing herself upright. She swayed across, a slim ghostly figure in the cloudy light. Harrison straddled the log and hitched himself ignominiously along.

He was too weary to trust *his* equilibrium. His feet dangled a foot or so above the black surface, and Celia, waiting impatiently on the further bank as she peered anxiously at the distant glow, cast him a look over her shoulder and cried a sudden urgent warning.

Harrison jerked up his legs just as something bulky and grisly heaved up out of the water with a great splash and an appalling clash of mighty fangs. Harrison fairly flung himself over the last few feet and landed on the further bank in a more demoralized condition than he would have admitted. A criminal in a dark room with a knife was less nerve-shaking than these ghoulish slayers of the dark waters.

The ground was firmer; they were, as Celia said, on a sort of island in the heart of the marshes. The girl threaded her supple way among the cypresses, panting with the intensity of her emotions. Perspiration soaked her; the hand that held Harrison's wrist was wet and slippery.

A few minutes later, when the glow in the trees had grown to an illuminating glare, she halted and slipped to the damp mold, drawing her companion with her. They looked out upon a scene incredible in its primitive starkness.

There was a clearing, free of underbrush, circled by a black wall of cypress. From its outer edge a sort of natural causeway wandered away into the gloom, and over that low ridge ran a trail, beaten by many feet. The trail ended in the clearing, the ultimate end of the path that Harrison had followed into the swamp. On the other side of the clearing there was a glimpse of dusky water, reflecting the firelight.

In a wide horseshoe formation, their backs to the causeway, sat some fifty men, women and children, resembling Celia Pompoloi in complexion. Harrison had not supposed that so many people inhabited the swamp. Their gaze was fixed on an object in the center of the opening of the human horseshoe. This was a great block of dark wood that had an unfamiliar appearance, as of an altar, brought from afar. There was an intolerable suggestion about that block, and the misshapen, leering figure that rose behind it—a fantastically carven idol, to whose bestial features the flickering firelight lent life and mobility. Harrison intuitively knew that this monstrosity was never carved in America. The yellow people had brought it with them from Haiti, and surely their black ancestors had brought it originally from Africa. There was an aura of the Congo about it, the reek of black squalling jungles, and squirming faceless shapes of a night more primeval than this. Harrison was not superstitious, but he felt gooseflesh rise on his limbs. At the back of his consciousness dim racial memories stirred, conjuring up unstable and monstrous images from the dim mists of the primitive, when men worshipped such gods as these.

Before the idol, near the block, sat an old crone, striking a bowl tom-tom with quick staccato strokes of her open hands; it growled and rumbled and muttered, and the squatting Negroes swayed and chanted softly in unison. Their voices were low, but they hummed with a note of hysteria. The fire struck gleams from their rolling eyeballs and shining teeth.

Harrison looked in vain for John Bartholomew and Woon Shang. He reached out a hand to get his companion's attention. She did not heed him. Her supple figure was tense and quivering as a taut wire under his hand. A sudden change in the chanting, a wild wolfish baying, brought him about again.

Out of the shadows of the trees behind the idol strode John Bartholomew. He was clad only in a loin cloth, and it was as if he had doffed his civilized culture with his clothing. His facial expression, his whole bearing, were changed; he was like an image of barbarism incarnate. Harrison stared at the knotted biceps, the ridged body muscles which the firelight displayed. But something else gripped his whole attention. With John Bartholomew came another, unwillingly, at the sight of whom the crowd gave tongue to another bestial yell.

About Bartholomew's mighty left hand was twisted the pigtail of Woon Shang, whom he dragged after him like a fowl to the chopping block. The Chinaman was stark naked, his yellow body gleaming like old ivory in the fire. His hands were bound behind his back, and he was like a child in the grasp of his executioner. Woon Shang was not a large man; beside the great mulatto he seemed slimmer than ever. His hysterical panting came plainly to Harrison in the silence that fell tensely as the shouting ceased and the Negroes watched with eyes that gleamed redly. His straining feet tore at the sod as he struggled against the inexorable advance of his captor. In Bartholomew's right hand shone a great razor-edged crescent of steel. The watchers sucked in their breath loudly; in a single stride they had returned to the jungle whence they had crawled; they were mad for the bloody saturnalia their ancestors had known.

In Bartholomew's face Harrison read stark horror and mad determination. He sensed that the mulatto was not enjoying this ghastly primordial drama into which be had been trapped. He also realized that the man must go through with it, and that he would go through with it. It was more than the jewel heart of the serpent-god for which Bartholomew strove now; it was the continued dominance of these wolfish devil-worshippers on which his life depended.

Harrison rose to one knee, drew and cocked his revolver and sighted along the blue barrel. The distance was not great, but the light was illusive. But he felt he must trust to the chance of sending a slug crashing through John Bartholomew's broad breast. If he stepped out into the open and tried to arrest the man, the Negroes, in their present fanatical frenzy, would tear him to pieces. If their priest was shot down, panic might seize them. His finger was crooking about the trigger when something was thrown into the fire. Abruptly the flames died down, throwing everything into deep shallow. As suddenly they flared up again, burning with a weird green radiance. The dusky faces looked like those of drowned corpses in the glow.

In the moment of darkness Bartholomew had reached the block. His victim's head was thrust down upon it, and the mulatto stood like a bronze image, his muscular right arm lifted, poising above his head the broad steel crescent. And then, before could strike the blow that would send Woon Shang's head rolling to the misshapen feet of the grinning idol, before Harrison could jerk the trigger, something froze them all in their places.

Into the weird glow moved a figure, so lithely that it seemed to float in the uncertain light rather than move on earthly feet. A groan burst from the Negroes, and they came to their feet like automatons. In the green glow that lent her features the aspect of death, with perspiration dripping from her draggled garment, Celia Pompoloi looked hideously like the corpse of a drowned woman newly risen from a watery grave.

"Celia!"

It was a scream from a score of gaping months. Bedlam followed.

"Celia Pompoloi! Oh Gawd, she done come back from de watah! Done come back from Hell!"

"Yes you dogs!" It was a most unghostly scream from Celia. "It's Celia Pompoloi, come back from Hell to send John Bartholomew there!"

And like a fury she rushed across the green-lit space, a knife she had found somewhere glittering in her hand. Bartholomew, momentarily paralyzed by the appearance of his prisoner, came to life. Releasing Woon Shang he stepped aside and swung the heavy beheading knife with all his power. Harrison saw the great muscles leap up under his glossy skin as he struck. But Celia's spring was that of a swamp panther. It carried her inside the circular sweep of the weighted blade, and her knife flashed as it sank to the hilt under John Bartholomew's heart. With a strangled cry he reeled and fell, dragging her down with him as she strove to wrench her blade free.

Abandoning it she rose, panting, her hair standing on end, her eyes starting from her head, her red lips writhing back in a curl of devilish rage. The people shrieked and gave back from her, still evidently in the grip of the delusion that they looked on one risen from the dead.

"Dogs!" she screamed, an incarnation of fury. "Fools! Swine! Have you lost your reason, to forget all my teachings, and let this dead dog make of you the beasts your fathers were? Oh—!" Glaring about for a weapon she caught up a blazing fire-brand and rushed at them, striking furiously. Men yelped as the flames bit them, and the sparks showered. Howling, cursing, and screaming they broke and fled, a frenzied mob, streaming out across the causeway, with their maddened priestess at their heels, screaming maledictions and smiting with the splintering fagot. They vanished in the darkness and their clamor came back faintly.

Harrison rose, shaking his head in wonder, and went stiffly up to the dying fire. Bartholomew was dead, staring glassily up at the moon which was breaking through the scattering clouds. Woon Shang crouched babbling incoherent Chinese as Harrison hauled him to his feet.

Woon Shang," said the detective wearily, "I arrest you for the murder of Li-keh-tsung. I warn you that anything you say will be used against you."

That formula seemed to invest the episode with some sanity, in contrast to the fantastic horror of the recent events. The Chinaman made no struggle. He seemed dazed, muttering: "This will break the heart of my honorable father; he had rather see me dead than dishonored."

"You ought to have thought of that before," said Harrison heavily. Through force of habit he cut Woon Shang's cords and reached for his handcuffs before he realized that they had been lost with his coat.

"Oh, well," he sighed. "I don't reckon you'll need them. Let's get going."

Laying a heavy hand on his captive's naked shoulder, Harrison half guided, half pushed him toward the causeway. The detective was dizzy with fatigue, but combined with it was a muddled determination to get his prisoner out of the swamp and into a jail before he stopped. He felt he had no more to fear from the swamp people, but he wanted to get out of that atmosphere of decay and slime in which he seemed to have been wandering for ages. Woon Shang took note of his condition with furtive side-long glances, as the stark fear died out of the Chinaman's beady black eyes to be replaced by one of craft.

"I have ten thousand dollars," be began babbling. "I hid it before the Negroes made me prisoner. I will give you all of it if you will let me go. . . ."

"Oh, shut up!" groaned Harrison wearily, giving him an exasperated shove. Woon Shang stumbled and went to his knees, his bare shoulder slipping from Harrison's grasp. The detective was stooping, fumbling for him when the Chinaman rose with a chunk of wood in his hand, and smote him savagely on the head. Harrison staggered back, almost falling, and Woon Shang, in a last desperate bid for freedom, dashed, not for the neck of land between which himself and Harrison stood, but straight toward the black water that glimmered beyond the fringe of cypresses. Harrison fired mechanically and without aim, but the fugitive kept straight on and hit the dusky water with a long dive.

Woon Shang's bobbing head was scarcely visible in the shadows of the overhanging ferns. Then a wild shriek cut the night; the water threshed and foamed, there was the glimpse of a writhing, horribly contorted yellow body and of a longer, darker shape, and then the blood-streaked waters closed over Woon Shang forever.

Harrison exhaled gustily and sank down on a rotting log.

"Well," he said wearily, aloud, "that winds *that* up. It's better this way. Woon's family had rather he died this way than in the chair, and they're decent folks, in spite of him. If this business had come to trial, I'd have had to tell about Celia shoving a knife into that devil Bartholomew, and I'd hate to see her on trial for killing that rat. This way it can be smoothed over. He had it coming to him. And I've got the money that's coming to old Li-keh-tsung's granddaughter. And it's me for the feather beds and fried steaks of civilization."

THE TOMB'S SECRET

When James Willoughby, millionaire philanthropist, realized that the dark, lightless car was deliberately crowding him into the curb, he acted with desperate decision. Snapping off his own lights, he threw open the door on the opposite side from the onrushing stranger, and leaped out, without stopping his own car. He landed sprawling on all fours, shredding the knees of his trousers and tearing the skin on his hands. An instant later his auto crashed cataclysmically into the curb, and the crunch of crumpled fenders and the tinkle of breaking glass mingled with the deafening reverberation of a sawed-off shotgun as the occupants of the mysterious car, not yet realizing that their intended victim had deserted his automobile, blasted the machine he had just left.

Before the echoes died away, Willoughby was up and running through the darkness with an energy remarkable for his years. He knew that his ruse was already discovered, but it takes longer to swing a big car around than for a desperately frightened man to burst through a hedge, and a flitting figure in the darkness is a poor target. So James Willoughby lived where others had died, and presently came on foot and in disheveled condition to his home, which adjoined the park beside which the murderous attempt had been made. The police, hastening to his call, found him in a condition of mingled fear and bewilderment. He had seen none of his attackers; he could give no reason for the attack. All that he seemed to know was that death had struck at him from the dark, suddenly, terribly and mysteriously.

It was only reasonable to suppose that death would strike again at its chosen victim, and that was why Brock Rollins, detective, kept a rendezvous the next evening with one Joey Glick, a nondescript character of the underworld who served his purpose in the tangled scheme of things.

Rollins bulked big in the dingy back-room appointed for the meeting. His massive shoulders and thick body dwarfed his height. His cold blue eyes contrasted with the thick black hair that crowned his low broad forehead, and his civilized garments could not conceal the almost savage muscularity of his hard frame.

Opposite him Joey Glick, never an impressive figure, looked even more insignificant than usual. And Joey's skin was a pasty grey, and Joey's fingers shook as he fumbled with a bit of paper on which was drawn a peculiar design.

"Somebody planted it on me," he chattered. "Right after I phoned you. In the jamb on the uptown train. Me, Joey Glick! They plant it on me and I don't even know it. Only one man in this burg handles dips that slick—even if I didn't know already.

"Look! It's the death-blossom! The symbol of the Sons of Erlik! They're after me! They've been shadowing me—tapping wires. They know I know too much—"

"Come to the point, will you?" grunted Rollins "You said you had a tip about the gorillas who tried to put the finger on Jim Willoughby. Quit shaking and spill it. And tell me, cold turkey—who was it?"

"The man behind it is Yarghouz Barolass."

Rollins grunted in some surprise.

"I didn't know murder was his racket."

"Wait!" Joey babbled, so scared he was scarcely coherent. His brain was addled, his speech disjointed. "He's head of the American branch of the Sons of Erlik—I know he is—"

"Chinese?"

"He's a Mongol. His racket is blackmailing nutty old dames who fall for his black magic. You know that. But this is bigger. Listen, you know about Richard Lynch?"

"Sure; got smashed up in an auto wreck by a hit-and-run speed maniac a week ago. Lay unidentified in a morgue all night before they discovered who he was. Some crazy loon tried to steal the corpse off the slab. What's that got to do with Willoughby?"

"It wasn't an accident." Joey was fumbling for a cigarette. "They meant to get him—Yarghouz's mob. It was them after the body that night—"

"Have you been hitting the pipe?" demanded Rollins harshly.

"No, damn it!" shrilled Joey. "I tell you, Yarghouz was after Richard Lynch's corpse, just like he's sending his mob after Job Hopkins' body tomorrow night—"

"*What?*" Rollins came erect, glaring incredulously.

"Don't rush me," begged Joey, striking a match. "Gimme time. That death-blossom has got me jumping sideways. I'm jittery—"

"I'll say you are," grunted Rollins. "You've been babbling a lot of stuff that don't mean anything, except it's Yarghouz Barolass who had Lynch bumped off, and now is after Willoughby. Why? That's what I want to know. Straighten it out and give me the low-down."

"Alright," promised Joey, sucking avidly at his cigarette. "Lemme have a drag. I been so upset I haven't even smoked since I reached into my pocket for a fag and found that damned death-flower. This is straight goods. I know why they want the bodies of Richard Lynch, Job Hopkins and James Willoughby—"

With appalling suddenness his hands shot to his throat, crushing the smoldering cigarette in his fingers. His eyes distended, his face purpled. Without a word he swayed upright, reeled and crashed to the floor. With a curse Rollins sprang up, bent over him, ran skilled hands over his body.

"Dead as Judas Iscariot," swore the detective. "What an infernal break! I knew his heart would get him some day, if he kept hitting the pipe—"

He halted suddenly. On the floor where it had fallen beside the dead man lay the bit of ornamented paper Joey had called the blossom of death, and beside it lay a crumpled package of cigarettes.

"When did he change his brand?" muttered Rollins. "He never smoked any kind but a special Egyptian make before; never saw him use this brand." He lifted the package, drew out a cigarette and broke it into his hand, smelling the contents gingerly. There was a faint but definite odor which was not part of the smell of the cheap tobacco.

"The fellow who slipped that death-blossom into his pocket could have shifted fags on him just as easy," muttered the detective. "They must have known he was coming here to talk to me. But the question is, how much do they know now? They can't know how much or how little he told me. They evidently didn't figure on him reaching me at all—thought he'd take a draw before he got here. Ordinarily he would have; but this time he was too scared even to remember to smoke. He needed dope, not tobacco, to steady his nerve."

Going to the door, he called softly. A stocky bald-headed man answered his call, wiping his hands on a dirty apron. At the sight of the crumpled body he recoiled, paling.

"Heart attack, Spike," grunted Rollins. "See that he gets what's needed." And the big dick thrust a handful of crumpled bills into Spike's fingers as he strode forth. A hard man, Rollins, but one mindful of his debts to the dead as well as the living.

A few minutes later be was crouched over a telephone.

"This you, Hoolihan?"

A voice booming back over the wires assured him that the chief of police was indeed at the other end.

"What killed Job Hopkins?" he asked abruptly.

"Why, heart attack, I understand." There was some surprise in the chief's voice. "Passed out suddenly, day before yesterday, while smoking his after-dinner cigar, according to the papers. Why?"

"Who's guarding Willoughby?" demanded Rollins without answering.

"Laveaux, Hanson, McFarlane and Harper. But I don't see—"

"Not enough," snapped Rollins. "Beat it over there yourself with three or four more men."

"Say, listen here, Rollins!" came back the irate bellow. "Are you telling *me* how to run my business?"

"Right now I am." Rollins' cold hard grin was almost tangible in his voice. "This happens to be in my particular domain. We're not fighting white men; it's a gang of River Street yellow-bellies who've put Willoughby on the spot. I won't say any more right now. There's been too damned much wire-tapping in this burg. But you beat it over to Willoughby's as fast as you can get there. Don't let him out of your sight. Don't let him smoke, eat or drink anything till I get there. I'll be right on over."

"Okay," came the answer over the wires. "You've been working the River Street quarter long enough to know what you're doing."

Rollins snapped the receiver back on its hook and strode out into the misty dimness of River Street, with its furtive hurrying forms—stooped alien figures which would have fitted less incongruously into the scheme of Canton, Bombay or Stamboul.

The big dick walked with a stride even springier than usual, a more aggressive lurch of his massive shoulders. That betokened unusual wariness, a tension of nerves. He knew that he was a marked man, since his talk with Joey Glick. He did not try to fool himself; it was certain that the spies of the man he was fighting knew that Joey had reached him before he died. The fact that they could not know just how much the fellow had told before he died, would make them all the more dangerous. He did not underestimate his own position. He knew that if there was one man in the city capable of dealing with Yarghouz Barolass, it was himself, with his experience gained from years of puzzling through the devious and often grisly mysteries of River Street, with its swarms of brown and yellow inhabitants.

"Taxi?" A cab drew purring up beside the curb, anticipating his summoning gesture. The driver did not lean out into the light of the street. His cap seemed to be drawn low, not unnaturally so, but, standing on the sidewalk, it was impossible for the detective to tell whether or not he was a white man.

"Sure," grunted Rollins, swinging open the door and climbing in. "540 Park Place, and step on it."

The taxi roared through the crawling traffic, down shadowy River Street, wheeled off onto 35th Avenue, crossed over, and sped down a narrow side street.

"Taking a short cut?" asked the detective.

"Yes, sir." The driver did not look back. His voice ended in a sudden hissing intake of breath. There was no partition between the front and back seats. Rollins was leaning forward, his gun jammed between the shoulders of the driver.

"Take the next right-hand turn and drive to the address I gave you," he said softly. "Think I can't tell the back of a yellow neck by the street lamp? You drive, but you drive careful. If you try to wreck us, I'll fill you full of lead before you can twist that wheel. No monkey business now; you wouldn't be the first man I've plugged in the course of duty."

The driver twisted his head about to stare briefly into the grim face of his captor; his wide thin mouth gaped, his coppery features were ashy. Not for nothing had Rollins established his reputation as a man-hunter among the sinister denizens of the Oriental quarter.

"Joey was right," muttered Rollins between his teeth. "I don't know your name, but I've seen you hanging around Yarghouz Barolass's joint when he had it over on Levant Street. You won't take me for a ride, not tonight. I know that trick, old copper-face. You'd have a flat, or run out of gas at some convenient spot. Any excuse for you to get out of the car and out of range while a hatchet-man hidden somewhere mows me down with a sawed-off. You better hope none of your friends see us and try anything, because this gat has a hair-trigger, and it's cocked. I couldn't die quick enough not to pull the trigger."

The rest of that grim ride was made in silence, until the reaches of South Park rose to view—darkened, except for a fringe of lights around the boundaries, because of municipal economy which sought to reduce the light bill.

"Swing into the park," ordered Rollins, as they drove along the street which passed the park, and, further on, James Willoughby's house. "Cut off your lights, and drive as I tell you. You can feel your way between the trees."

The darkened car glided into a dense grove and came to a halt. Rollins fumbled in his pockets with his left hand and drew out a small flashlight, and a pair of handcuffs. In climbing out, he was forced to remove his muzzle from close contact with his prisoner's back, but the gun menaced the Mongol in the small ring of light emanating from the flash.

"Climb out," ordered the detective. "That's right—slow and easy. You're going to have to stay here awhile. I didn't want to take you to the station right now, for several reasons. One of them is I didn't want your pals to know I turned the tables on you. I'm hoping they'll still be patiently waiting for you to bring me into range of their sawed-offs—ha, would you?"

The Mongol, with a desperate wrench, struck the flashlight from the detective's hand, plunging them into darkness.

Rollins' clutching fingers locked like a vise on his adversary's coat sleeve, and at the same instant he instinctively threw out his .45 before his belly, to parry the stroke he knew would instantly come. A knife clashed venomously against the blue steel cylinder, and Rollins hooked his foot about an ankle and jerked powerfully. The fighters went down together, and the knife sliced the detective's coat as they fell. Then his blindingly driven gun barrel crunched glancingly against a shaven skull, and the straining form went limp.

Panting and swearing beneath his breath, Rollins retrieved the flashlight and cuffs, and set to work securing his prisoner. The Mongol was completely out; it was no light matter to stop a full-arm swing from Brock Rollins. Had the blow landed solidly it would have caved in the skull like an egg-shell.

Handcuffed, gagged with strips torn from his coat, and his feet bound with the same material, the Mongol was placed in the car, and Rollins turned and strode through the shadows of the park, toward the eastern hedge beyond which lay James Willoughby's estate. He hoped that this affair would give him some slight advantage in this blind battle. While the Mongols waited for him to ride into the trap they had undoubtedly laid for him somewhere in the city, perhaps he could do a little scouting unmolested.

James Willoughby's estate adjoined South Park on the east. Only a high hedge separated the park from his grounds. The big three-storied house—disproportionately huge for a bachelor—towered among carefully trimmed trees and shrubbery, amidst a level, shaven lawn. There were lights in the two lower floors, none in the third. Rollins knew that Willoughby's study was a big room on the second floor, on the west side of the house. From that room no light issued between the heavy shutters. Evidently curtains and shades were drawn inside. The big dick grunted in approval as he stood looking through the hedge.

He knew that a plainclothes man was watching the house from each side, and he marked the bunch of shrubbery amidst which would be crouching the man detailed to guard the west side. Craning his neck, he saw a car in front of the house, which faced south, and he knew it to be that of Chief Hoolihan.

With the intention of taking a short cut across the lawn he wormed through the hedge, and, not wishing to be shot by mistake, he called softly: "Hey, Harper!"

There was no answer. Rollins strode toward the shrubbery.

"Asleep at the post?" he muttered angrily. "Eh, what's this?"

He had stumbled over something in the shadows of the shrubs. His hurriedly directed beam shone on the white, upturned face of a man. Blood dabbled the features, and a crumpled hat lay near by, an unfired pistol near the limp hand.

"Knocked stiff from behind!" muttered Rollins. "What—"

Parting the shrub he gazed toward the house. On that side an ornamental chimney rose tier by tier, until it towered above the roof. And his eyes became slits as they centered on a window on the third floor within easy reach of that chimney. On all other windows the shutters were closed; but these stood open.

With frantic haste he tore through the shrubbery and ran across the lawn, stooping like a bulky bear, amazingly fleet for one of his weight. As he rounded the corner of the house and rushed toward the steps, a man rose swiftly from among the hedges lining the walk, and covered him, only to lower his gun with an exclamation of recognition.

Where's Hoolihan?" snapped the detective.

"Upstairs with old man Willoughby. What's up?"

"Harper's been slugged," snarled Rollins. "Beat it out there; you know where he was posted. Wait there until I call you. If you see anything you don't recognize trying to leave the house, plug it! I'll send out a man to take your place here."

He entered the front door and saw four men in plain clothes lounging about in the main hall.

"Jackson," he snapped, "take Hanson's place out in front. I sent him around to the west side. The rest of you stand by for anything."

Mounting the stair in haste, he entered the study on the second floor, breathing a sigh of relief as he found the occupants apparently undisturbed.

The curtains were closely drawn over the windows, and only the door letting into the hall was open. Willoughby was there, a tall spare man, with a scimitar sweep of nose and a bony aggressive chin. Chief Hoolihan, big, bear-like, rubicund, boomed a greeting.

"All your men downstairs?" asked Rollins.

"Sure; nothin' can get past 'em and I'm stayin' here with Mr. Willoughby—"

"And in a few minutes more you'd both have been scratching gravel in Hell," snapped Rollins. "Didn't I tell you we were dealing with Orientals? You concentrated all your force below, never thinking that death might slip in on you from above. But I haven't time to turn out that light. Mr. Willoughby, get over there in that alcove. Chief, stand in front of him, and watch that door that leads into the hall. I'm going to leave it open. Locking it would be useless, against what we're fighting. If anything you don't recognize comes through it, shoot to kill."

"What the devil are you driving at, Rollins?" demanded Hoolihan.

"I mean one of Yarghouz Barolass's killers is in this house!" snapped Rollins. "There may be more than one; anyway, he's somewhere upstairs. Is this the only stair, Mr. Willoughby? No back-stair?"

"This is the only one in the house," answered the millionaire. "There are only bedrooms on the third floor."

"Where's the light button for the hall on that floor?"

"At the head of the stairs, on the left; but you aren't—"

"Take your places and do as I say," grunted Rollins, gliding out into the hallway.

He stood glaring at the stair which wound up above him, its upper part masked in shadow. Somewhere up there lurked a soulless slayer—a Mongol killer, trained in the art of murder, who lived only to perform his master's will. Rollins started to call the men below, then changed his mind. To raise his voice would be to warn the lurking murderer above. Setting his teeth, he glided up the stair. Aware that he was limned in the light below, he realized the desperate recklessness of his action; but he had long ago learned that he could not match subtlety against the Orient. Direct action, however desperate, was always his best bet. He did not fear a bullet as he charged up; the Mongols preferred to slay in silence; but a thrown knife could kill as promptly as tearing lead. His one chance lay in the winding of the stair.

He took the last steps with a thundering rush, not daring to use his flash, plunged into the gloom of the upper hallway, frantically sweeping the wall for the light button. Even as he felt life and movement in the darkness beside him, his groping fingers found it. The scrape of a foot on the floor beside him galvanized him, and as he instinctively flinched back, something whined past his breast and thudded deep into the wall. Then under his frenzied fingers, light flooded the hall.

Almost touching him, half crouching, a copper-skinned giant with a shaven head wrenched at a curved knife which was sunk deep in the woodwork. He threw up his head, dazzled by the light, baring yellow fangs in a bestial snarl.

Rollins had just left a lighted area. His eyes accustomed themselves more swiftly to the sudden radiance. He threw his left like a hammer at the Mongol's jaw. The killer swayed and fell out cold.

Hoolilhan was bellowing from below.

"Hold everything," answered Rollins. "Send one of the boys up here with the cuffs. I'm going through these bedrooms."

Which he did, switching on the lights, gun ready, but finding no other lurking slayer. Evidently Yarghouz Barolass considered one would be enough. And so it might have been, but for the big detective.

Having latched all the shutters and fastened the windows securely, he returned to the study, whither the prisoner had been taken. The man had recovered his senses and sat, handcuffed, on a divan. Only the eyes, black and snaky, seemed alive in the copperish face.

"Mongol alright," muttered Rollins. "No Chinaman."

"What is all this?" complained Hoolihan, still upset by the realization that an invader had slipped through his cordon.

"Easy enough. This fellow sneaked up on Harper and laid him cold. Some of these fellows could steal the teeth right out of your mouth. With all those shrubs and trees it was a cinch. Say, send out a couple of the boys to bring in Harper, will you? Then he climbed that fancy chimney. That was a cinch, too. I could do it myself. Nobody had thought to fasten the shutters on that floor, because nobody expected an attack from that direction.

"Mr. Willoughby, do you know anything about Yarghouz Barolass?"

"I never heard of him," declared the philanthropist, and though Rollins scanned him narrowly, he was impressed by the ring of sincerity in Willoughby's voice.

"Well, he's a mystic fakir," said Rollins. "Hangs around Levant Street and preys on old ladies with more money than sense—faddists.

Gets them interested in Taoism and Lamaism and then plays on their superstitions and blackmails them. I know his racket, but I've never been able to put the finger on him, because his victims won't squeal. But he's behind these attacks on you."

"Then why don't we go grab him?" demanded Hoolihan.

"Because we don't know where he is. He knows that I know he's mixed up in this. Joey Glick spilled it to me, just before he croaked. Yes, Joey's dead—poison; more of Yarghouz's work. By this time Yarghouz will have deserted his usual hang-outs, and be hiding some-where—probably in some secret underground dive that we couldn't find in a hundred years, now that Joey is dead."

"Let's sweat it out of this yellow-belly," suggested Hoolihan.

Rollins grinned coldly. "You'd sweat to death yourself before he'd talk. There's another tied up in a car out in the park. Send a couple of boys after him, and you can try your hand on both of them. But you'll get damned little out of them. Come here, Hoolihan."

Drawing him aside, he said: "I'm sure that Job Hopkins was poi-soned in the same manner they got Joey Glick. Do you remember any-thing unusual about the death of Richard Lynch?"

"Well, not about his death; but that night somebody apparently tried to steal and mutilate his corpse—"

"What do you mean, mutilate?" demanded Rollins.

"Well, a watchman heard a noise and went into the room and found Lynch's body on the floor, as if somebody had tried to carry it off, and then maybe got scared off. And a lot of the *teeth* had been pulled or knocked out!"

"Well, I can't explain the teeth," grunted Rollins. "Maybe they were knocked out in the wreck that killed Lynch. But this is my hunch: Yarghouz Barolass is stealing the bodies of wealthy men, figuring on screwing a big price out of their families. When they don't die quick enough, he bumps them off."

Hoolihan cursed in shocked horror.

"But Willoughby hasn't any family."

"Well, I reckon they figure the executors of his estate will kick in. Now listen: I'm borrowing your car for a visit to Job Hopkins' vault. I got a tip that they're going to lift his corpse tomorrow night. I believe they'll spring it tonight, on the chance that I might have gotten the tip. I believe they'll try to get ahead of me. They may have already, what with all this delay. I figured on being out there long before now.

"No, I don't want any help. Your flat-feet are more of a hindrance than a help in a job like this. You stay here with Willoughby. Keep men upstairs as well as down. Don't let Willoughby open any packages that might come, don't even let him answer a phone call. I'm going to Hopkins' vault, and I don't know when I'll be back; may roost out there all night. It just depends on when—or if—they come for the corpse."

A few minutes later he was speeding down the road on his grim errand. The graveyard which contained the tomb of Job Hopkins was small, exclusive, where only the bones of rich men were laid to rest. The wind moaned through the cypress trees which bent shadow-arms above the gleaming marble.

Rollins approached from the back side, up a narrow, tree-lined side street. He left the car, climbed the wall, and stole through the gloom, beneath the pallid shafts, under the cypress shadows. Ahead of him Job Hopkins' tomb glimmered whitely. And he stopped short, crouching low in the shadows. He saw a glow—a spark of light—it was extinguished, and through the open door of the tomb trooped half a dozen shadowy forms. His hunch had been right, but they had gotten there ahead of him. Fierce anger sweeping him at the ghoulish crime, he leaped forward, shouting a savage command.

They scattered like rats, and his crashing volley re-echoed futilely among the sepulchers. Rushing forward recklessly, swearing savagely, he came into the tomb, and turning his light into the interior, winced at what he saw. The coffin had been burst open, but the tomb itself was not empty. In a careless heap on the floor lay the embalmed corpse of Job Hopkins—*and the lower jawbone had been sawed away.*

"What the Hell!" Rollins stopped short, bewildered at the sudden disruption of his theory. "They didn't want the body. What did they want? His teeth? And they got Richard Lynch's teeth—"

Lifting the body back into its resting place, he hurried forth, shutting the door of the tomb behind him. The wind whined through the cypress, and mingled with it was a low moaning sound. Thinking that one of his shots had gone home, after all, he followed the noise, warily, pistol and flash ready.

The sound seemed to emanate from a bunch of low cedars near the wall, and among them he found a man lying. The beam revealed the stocky figure, the square, now convulsed face of a Mongol. The slant eyes were glazed, the back of the coat soaked with blood. The man was gasping his last, but Rollins found no trace of a bullet wound on him. In his back, between his shoulders, stood up the hilt of a curious skewer-like knife. The fingers of his right hand had been horribly gashed, as if he had sought to retain his grasp on something which his slayers desired.

"Running from me he bumped into somebody hiding among these cedars," muttered Rollins. "But who? And why? By God, Willoughby hasn't told me everything."

He stared uneasily at the crowding shadows. No stealthy shuffling footfall disturbed the sepulchral quiet. Only the wind whimpered through the cypress and the cedars. The detective was alone with the dead—with the corpses of rich men in their ornate tombs, and with the staring yellow man whose flesh was not yet rigid.

"You're back in a hurry," said Hoolihan, as Rollins entered the Willoughby study. "Do any good?"

"Did the yellow boys talk?" countered Rollins.

"They did not," growled the chief. "They sat like pot-bellied idols. I sent 'em to the station, along with Harper. He was still in a daze."

"Mr. Willoughby," Rollins sank down rather wearily into an armchair and fixed his cold gaze on the philanthropist, "am I right in believing that you and Richard Lynch and Job Hopkins were at one time connected with each other in some way?"

"Why do you ask?" parried Willoughby.

"Because somehow the three of you are connected in this matter. Lynch's death was not accidental, and I'm pretty sure that Job Hopkins was poisoned. Now the same gang is after you. I thought it was a body-snatching racket, but an apparent attempt to steal Richard Lynch's corpse out of the morgue, now seems to resolve itself into what was in reality a successful attempt to get his teeth. Tonight a gang of Mongols entered the tomb of Job Hopkins, obviously for the same purpose—"

A choking cry interrupted him. Willoughby sank back, his face livid.

"My God, after all these years!"

Rollins stiffened.

"Then you do know Yarghouz Barolass? You know why he's after you?"

Willoughby shook his head. "I never heard of Yarghouz Barolass before. But I know why they killed Lynch and Hopkins."

"Then you'd better spill the works," advised Rollins. "We're working in the dark as it is."

"I will!" The philanthropist was visibly shaken. He mopped his brow with a shaking hand, and reposed himself with an effort.

"Twenty years ago," he said, "Lynch, Hopkins and myself, young men just out of college, were in China, in the employ of the war-lord Yuen Chin. We were chemical engineers. Yuen Chin was a far-sighted man—ahead of his time, scientifically speaking. He visioned the day when men would war with gases and deadly chemicals. He supplied us with a splendid laboratory, in which to discover or invent some such element of destruction for his use.

"He paid us well; the foundations of all of our fortunes were laid there. We were young, poor, unscrupulous.

"More by chance than skill we stumbled onto a deadly secret—the formula for a poisonous gas, a thousand times more deadly than anything yet dreamed of. That was what he was paying us to invent or discover for him, but the discovery sobered us. We realized that the man who possessed the secret of that gas, could easily conquer the world. We were willing to aid Yuen Chin against his Mongolian enemies; we were not willing to elevate a yellow mandarin to world empire, to see our hellish discovery directed against the lives of our own people.

"Yet we were not willing to destroy the formula, because we foresaw a time when America, with her back to the wall, might have a desperate need for such a weapon. So we wrote out the formula in code, but left out three symbols, without any of which the formula is meaningless and undecipherable. Each of us then, had a lower jaw tooth pulled out, and on the gold tooth put in its place, was carved one of the three symbols. Thus we took precautions against our own greed, as well as against the avarice of outsiders. One of us might conceivably fall so low as to sell the secret, but it would be useless without the other two symbols.

"Yuen Chin fell and was beheaded on the great execution ground at Peking. We escaped, Lynch, Hopkins and I, not only with our lives but with most of the money which had been paid us. But the formula, scrawled on parchment, we were obliged to leave, secreted among musty archives in an ancient temple.

"Only one man knew our secret: an old Chinese tooth-puller, who aided us in the matter of the teeth. He owed his life to Richard Lynch, and when he swore the oath of eternal silence, we knew we could trust him."

"Yet you think somebody is after the secret symbols?"

"What else could it be? I cannot understand it. The old tooth-puller must have died long ago. Who could have learned of it? Torture would not have dragged the secret from him. Yet it can be for no other reason that this fellow you call Yarghouz Barolass murdered and mutilated the bodies of my former companions, and now is after me.

"Why, I love life as well as any man, but my own peril shrinks into insignificance compared to the world-wide menace contained in those little carven symbols—two of which are now, according to what you say, in the hands of some ruthless foe of the western world.

"Somebody has found the formula we left hidden in the temple, and has learned somehow of its secret. Anything can come out of China. Just now the bandit war-lord Yah Lai is threatening to over-throw the National government—who knows what devilish concoc-tion that Chinese caldron is brewing?

"The thought of the secret of that gas in the hands of some Orien-tal conqueror is appalling. My God, gentlemen, I fear you do not real-ize the full significance of the matter!"

"I've got a faint idea," grunted Rollins. "Ever see a dagger like this?" He presented the weapon that had killed the Mongol.

"Many of them, in China," answered Willoughby promptly.

"Then it isn't a Mongol weapon?"

"No; it's distinctly Chinese; there is a conventional Manchu inscription on the hilt."

"Ummmmmm!" Rollins sat scowling, chin on fist, idly tapping the blade against his shoe, lost in meditation. Admittedly, he was all at sea, lost in a bewildering tangle. To his companions he looked like a grim figure of retribution, brooding over the fate of the wicked. In reality he was cursing his luck.

"What are you going to do now?" demanded Hoolihan.

"Only one thing to do," responded Rollins. "I'm going to try to run down Yarghouz Barolass. I'm going to start with River Street—God knows, it'll be like looking for a rat in a swamp. I want you to contrive to let one of those Mongols escape, Hoolihan. I'll try to trail him back to Yarghouz's hangout—"

The phone tingled loudly.

Rollins reached it with a long stride.

"Who speaks, please?" Over the wire came a voice with a subtle but definite accent.

"Brock Rollins," grunted the big dick.

"A friend speaks, Detective," came the bland voice. "Before we progress further, let me warn you that it will be impossible to trace this call, and would do you no good to do so."

"Well?" Rollins was bristling like a big truculent dog.

"Mr. Willoughby," the suave voice continued, "is a doomed man. He is as good as dead already. Guards and guns will not save him, when the Sons of Erlik are ready to strike. But *you* can save him, without firing a shot!"

"Yeah?" It was a scarcely articulate snarl humming bloodthirstily from Rollins' bull-throat.

"If you were to come alone to the House of Dreams on Levant street, Yarghouz Barolass would speak to you, and a compromise might be arranged whereby Mr. Willoughby's life would be spared."

"Compromise, Hell!" roared the big dick, the skin over his knuckles showing white. "Who do you think you're talking to? Think I'd fall into a trap like that?"

"You have a hostage," came back the voice. "One of the men you hold is Yarghouz Barolass's brother. Let him suffer if there is treachery. I swear by the bones of my ancestors, no harm shall come to you!"

The voice ceased with a click at the other end of the wire.

Rollins wheeled.

"Yarghouz Barolass must be getting desperate to try such a child's trick as that!" he swore. Then he considered, and muttered, half to himself: "By the bones of his ancestors! Never heard of a Mongolian breaking *that* oath. All that stuff about Yarghouz's brother may be the bunk. Yet—well, maybe he's trying to outsmart me—draw me away from Willoughby—on the other hand, maybe he thinks that I'd never fall for a trick like that—aw, to Hell with thinking! I'm going to start acting!"

"What do you mean?" demanded Hoolihan.

"I mean I'm going to the House of Dreams, alone."

"You're crazy!" exclaimed Hoolihan. "Take a squad, surround the house, and raid it!"

"And find an empty rat-den," grunted Rollins, his peculiar obsession for working alone again asserting itself.

Dawn was not far away when Rollins entered the smoky den near the waterfront which was known to the Chinese as the House of Dreams, and whose dingy exterior masked a subterranean opium joint. Only a pudgy Chinaboy nodded behind the counter; he looked up with no apparent surprise. Without a word he led Rollins to a curtain in the back of the shop, pulled it aside, and revealed a door. The detective gripped his gun under his coat, nerves taut with excitement that must come to any man who has deliberately walked into what might prove to be a death-trap. The boy knocked, lifting a sing-song monotone, and a voice answered from within. Rollins started. He recognized that voice. The boy opened the door, bobbed his head and was gone. Rollins entered, pulling the door to behind him.

He was in a room heaped and strewn with divans and silk cushions. If there were other doors, they were masked by the black velvet hangings, which, worked with gilt dragons, covered the walls. On a divan near the further wall squatted a stocky, pot-bellied shape, in black silk, a close-fitting velvet cap on his shaven head.

"So you came, after all!" breathed the detective. "Don't move, Yarghouz Barolass. I've got you covered through my coat. Your gang can't get me quick enough to keep me from getting you first."

"Why do you threaten me, Detective?" Yarghouz Barolass's face was expressionless, the square, parchment-skinned face of a Mongol from the Gobi, with wide thin lips and glittering black eyes. His English was perfect.

"See, I trust you. I am here, alone. The boy who let you in said that you are alone. Good. You kept your word, I keep my promise. For the time there is truce between us, and I am ready to bargain, as you suggested."

"As *I* suggested?" demanded Rollins.

"I have no desire to harm Mr. Willoughby, any more than I wished to harm either of the other gentlemen," said Yarghouz Barolass. "But knowing them all as I did—from report and discreet observation—it never occurred to me that I could obtain what I wished while they lived. So I did not enter into negotiations with them."

"So you want Willoughby's tooth, too?"

"Not I," disclaimed Yarghouz Barolass. "It is an honorable person in China, the grandson of an old man who babbled in his dotage, as old men often do, drooling secrets torture could not have wrung from him in his soundness of mind. The grandson, Yah Lai, has risen from a mean position to that of war-lord. He listened to the mumblings of his grandfather, a tooth-puller. He found a formula, written in code, and learned of symbols on the teeth of old men. He sent a request to me, with promise of much reward. I have one tooth, procured from the unfortunate person, Richard Lynch. Now if you will hand over the other—that of Job Hopkins—as you promised, perhaps we may reach a compromise by which Mr. Willoughby will be allowed to keep his life, in return for a tooth, as you hinted."

"As *I* hinted?" exclaimed Rollins. "What are you driving at? I made no promise; and I certainly haven't Job Hopkins' tooth. You've got it, yourself."

"All this is unnecessary," objected Yarghouz, an edge to his tone. "You have a reputation for veracity, in spite of your violent nature. I was relying upon your reputation for honesty when I accepted this appointment. Of course, I already knew that you had Hopkins' tooth. When my blundering servants, having been frightened by you as they left the vaults, gathered at the appointed rendezvous, they discovered that he to whom was entrusted the jaw-bone containing the precious tooth, was not among them. They returned to the graveyard and found his body, but not the tooth. It was obvious that you had killed him and taken it from him."

Rollins was so thunderstruck by this new twist, that he remained speechless, his mind a tangled whirl of bewilderment.

Yarghouz Barolass continued tranquilly: "I was about to send my servants out in another attempt to secure you, when your agent phoned me—though how he located me on the telephone is still a mystery into which I must inquire—and announced that you were ready to meet me at the House of Dreams, and give me Job Hopkins' tooth, in return for an opportunity to bargain personally for Mr. Willoughby's life. Knowing you to be a man of honor, I agreed, trusting you—"

"This is madness!" exclaimed Rollins "I didn't call you, or have anybody call you. *You,* or rather, one of your men, called *me.*"

"I did not!" Yarghouz was on his feet, his stocky body under the rippling black silk quivering with rage and suspicion. His eyes narrowed to slits, his wide mouth knotted viciously.

"You deny that you promised to give me Job Hopkins' tooth?"

"Sure I do!" snapped Rollins. "I haven't got it, and what's more, I'm not 'compromising' as you call it—"

"Liar!" Yarghouz spat the epithet like a snake hissing. "You have tricked—betrayed me—used my trust in your blackened honor to dupe me—"

"Keep cool," advised Rollins. "Remember, I've got a Colt .45 trained on you."

"Shoot and die!" retorted Yarghouz. "I do not know what your game is, but I know that if you shoot me, we will fall together. Fool, do you think I would keep my promise to a barbarian dog? Behind this hanging is the entrance to a tunnel through which I can escape before any of your stupid police, if you have brought any with you, can enter this room. You have been covered since you came through that door, by a man hiding behind the tapestry. Try to stop me, and you die!"

"I believe you're telling the truth about not calling me," said Rollins slowly. "I believe somebody tricked us both, for some reason. You were called, in my name, and I was called, in yours."

Yarghouz halted short in some hissing tirade. His eyes were like black evil jewels in the lamplight.

"More lies?" he demanded uncertainly.

"No; I think somebody in your gang is double-crossing you. Now easy, I'm not pulling a gun. I'm just going to show you the knife that I found sticking in the back of the fellow you seem to think I killed."

He drew it from his coat-pocket with his left hand—his right still gripped his gun beneath the garment—and tossed it on the divan.

Yarghouz pounced on it. His slit eyes flared wide with a terrible light; his yellow skin went ashen. He cried out something in his own tongue, which Rollins did not understand.

In a torrent of hissing sibilances, he lapsed briefly into English: "I see it all now! This was too subtle for a barbarian! Death to them all!" Wheeling toward the tapestry behind the divan he shrieked: "Gutchluk!"

There was no answer, but Rollins thought he saw the black velvety expanse billow slightly. With his skin the color of old ashes, Yarghouz Barolass ran at the hanging, ignoring Rollins' order to halt, seized the tapestries, tore them aside—something flashed between them like a beam of white hot light. Yarghouz's scream broke in a ghastly gurgle. His head pitched forward, then his whole body swayed backward, and he fell heavily among the cushions, clutching at the hilt of a skewer-like dagger that quivered upright in his breast. The Mongol's yellow claw-like hands fell away from the crimsoned hilt, spread wide, clutching at the thick carpet; a convulsive spasm ran through his frame, and those taloned yellow fingers went limp.

Gun in hand, Rollins took a single stride toward the tapestries—then halted short, staring at the figure which moved imperturbably through them: a tall yellow man in the robes of a mandarin, who smiled and bowed, his hands hidden in his wide sleeves.

"You killed Yarghous Barolass!" accused the detective.

The evil one indeed has been dispatched to join his ancestors by my hand," agreed the mandarin. "Be not afraid. The Mongol who covered you through a peep-hole with an abbreviated shotgun has likewise departed this uncertain life, suddenly and silently. My own people hold supreme in the House of Dreams this night. All that we ask is that you make no attempt to stay our departure."

"Who are you?" demanded Rollins.

"But a humble servant of Fang Yin, lord of Peking. When it was learned that these unworthy ones sought a formula in America that might enable the upstart Yah Lai to overthrow the government of China, word was sent in haste to me. It was almost too late. Two men had already died. The third was menaced.

"I sent my servants instantly to intercept the evil Sons of Erlik at the vaults they desecrated. But for your appearance, frightening the Mongols to scattering in flight, before the trap could be sprang, my servants would have caught them all in ambush. As it was, they did manage to slay he who carried the relic Yarghouz sought, and this they brought to me.

"I took the liberty of impersonating a servant of the Mongol in my speech with you, and of pretending to be a Chinese agent of yours, while speaking with Yarghouz. All worked out as I wished. Lured by the thought of the tooth, at the loss of which he was maddened, Yarghouz came from his secret, well-guarded lair, and fell into my hands. I brought you here to witness his execution, so that you might realize that Mr. Willoughby is no longer in danger. Fang Yin has no ambitions for world empire; he wishes but to hold what is his. That he is well able to do, now that the threat of the devil-gas is lifted. And now I must be gone. Yarghouz had laid careful plans for his flight out of the country. I will take advantage of his preparations."

"Wait a minute!" exclaimed Rollins. "I've got to arrest you for the murder of this rat."

"I am sorry," murmured the mandarin. "I am in much haste. No need to lift your revolver. I swore that you would not be injured and I keep my word."

As he spoke, the light went suddenly out. Rollins sprang forward, cursing, fumbling at the tapestries which had swished in the darkness as if from the passing of a large body between them. His fingers met only solid walls, and when at last the light came on again, he was alone in the room, and behind the hangings a heavy door had been slid shut. On the divan lay something that glinted in the lamplight, and Rollins looked down on a curiously carven gold tooth.

NAMES IN THE BLACK BOOK

Three unsolved murders in a week are not so unusual—for River Street," grunted Steve Harrison, shifting his muscular bulk restlessly in his chair.

His companion lighted a cigarette and Harrison observed that her slim hand was none too steady. She was exotically beautiful, a dark, supple figure, with the rich colors of purple Eastern nights and crimson dawns in her dusky hair and red lips. But in her dark eyes Harrison glimpsed the shadow of fear. Only once before had he seen fear in those marvelous eyes, and the memory made him vaguely uneasy.

"It's your business to solve murders," she said.

"Give me a little time. You can't rush things, when you're dealing with the people of the Oriental quarter."

"You have less time than you think," she answered cryptically. "If you do not listen to me, you'll never solve these killings."

"I'm listening."

"But you won't believe. You'll say I'm hysterical—seeing ghosts and shying at shadows."

"Look here, Joan," he exclaimed impatiently. "Come to the point. You called me to your apartment and I came because you said you were in deadly danger. But now you're talking riddles about three men who were killed last week. Spill it plain, won't you?"

"Do you remember Erlik Khan?" she asked abruptly.

Involuntarily his hand sought his face, where a thin scar ran from temple to jaw-rim.

"I'm not likely to forget him," he said. "A Mongol who called himself Lord of the Dead. His idea was to combine all the Oriental criminal societies in America in one big organization, with himself at the head. He might have done it, too, if his own men hadn't turned on him."

"Erlik Khan has returned," she said.

"What!" His head jerked up and he glared at her incredulously. "What are you talking about? I saw him die, and so did you!"

"I saw his hood fall apart as Ali ibn Suleyman struck with his keen-edged scimitar," she answered. "I saw him roll to the floor and lie still. And then the house went up in flames, and the roof fell in, and only charred bones were ever found among the ashes. Nevertheless, Erlik Khan has returned."

Harrison did not reply, but sat waiting for further disclosures, sure they would come in an indirect way. Joan La Tour was half Oriental, and partook of many of the characteristics of her subtle kin.

"How did those three men die?" she asked, though he was aware that she knew as well as he.

"Li-crin, the Chinese merchant, fell from his own roof," he grunted. The people on the street heard him scream and then saw him come hurtling down. Might have been an accident—but middle-aged Chinese merchants don't go climbing around on roofs at midnight.

"Ibrahim ibn Achmet, the Syrian curio dealer, was bitten by a cobra. That might have been an accident too, only I know somebody dropped the snake on him through his skylight.

"Jacob Kossova, the Levantine exporter, was simply knifed in a back alley. Dirty jobs, all of them, and no apparent motive on the surface. But motives are hidden deep, in River Street. When I find the guilty parties I'll uncover the motives."

"And these murders suggest nothing to you?" exclaimed the girl, tense with suppressed excitement. "You do not see the link that connects them? You do not grasp the point they all have in common? Listen—all these men were formerly associated in one way or another with Erlik Khan!"

"Well?" he demanded. "That doesn't mean that the Khan's spook killed them! We found plenty of bones in the ashes of the house, but there were members of his gang in other parts of the city. His gigantic organization went to pieces, after his death, for lack of a leader, but the survivors were never uncovered. Some of them might be paying off old grudges."

"Then why did they wait so long to strike? It's been a year since we saw Erlik Khan die. I tell you, the Lord of the Dead himself, alive or dead, has returned and is striking down these men for one reason or another. Perhaps they refuse to do his bidding once more. Five were marked for death. Three have fallen."

"How do you know that?" said he.

"Look!" From beneath the cushions of the divan on which she sat she drew something, and rising, came and bent beside him while she unfolded it.

It was a square piece of parchment-like substance, black and glossy. On it were written five names, one below the other, in a bold flowing hand—and in crimson, like spilled blood. Through the first three names a crimson bar had been drawn. They were the names of Li-chin, Ibrahim ibn Achmet, and Jacob Kossova. Harrison grunted explosively. The last two names, as yet unmarred, were those of Joan La Tour and Stephen Harrison.

"Where did you get this?" he demanded.

"It was shoved under my door last night, while I slept. If all the doors and windows had not been locked, the police would have found it pinned to my corpse this morning."

"But still I don't see what connection—"

"It is a page from the Black Book of Erlik Khan!" she cried. "The book of the dead! I have seen it, when I was a subject of his in the old days. There he kept accounts of his enemies, alive and dead. I saw that book, open, the very day of the night Ali ibn Suleyman killed him—a big book with jade-hinged ebony covers and glossy black parchment pages. Those names were not in it then; they have been written in since Erlik Khan died—and that is Erlik Khan's handwriting!"

If Harrison was impressed he failed to show it.

"Does he keep his books in English?"

"No, in a Mongolian script. This is for our benefit. And I know we are hopelessly doomed. Erlik Khan never warned his victims unless he was sure of them."

"Might be a forgery," grunted the detective.

"No! No man could imitate Erlik Khan's hand. He wrote those names himself. He has come back from the dead! Hell could not hold a devil as black as he!" Joan was losing some of her poise in her fear and excitement. She ground out the half-consumed cigarette and broke the cover of a fresh carton. She drew forth a slim white cylinder and tossed the package on the table. Harrison took it up and absently extracted one for himself.

"Our names are in the Black Book! It is a sentence of death from which there is no appeal!" She struck a match and was lifting it, when Harrison struck the cigarette from her with a startled oath. She fell back on the divan, bewildered at the violence of his action, and he caught up the package and began gingerly to remove the contents.

"Where'd you get these things?"

"Why, down at the corner drug store, I guess," she stammered. "That's where I usually—"

"Not these you didn't," he grunted. "These fags have been specially treated. I don't know what it is, but I've seen one puff of the stuff knock a man stone dead. Some kind of a hellish Oriental drug mixed with the tobacco. You were out of your apartment while you were phoning me—"

"I was afraid my wire was tapped," she answered. "I went to a public booth down the street."

"And it's my guess somebody entered your apartment while you were gone and switched cigarettes on you. I only got a faint whiff of the stuff when I started to put that fag in my mouth, but it's unmistakable. Smell it yourself. Don't be afraid. It's deadly only when ignited."

She obeyed, and turned pale.

"I told you! We were the direct cause of Erlik Khan's overthrow! If you hadn't smelt that drug, we'd both be dead now, as he intended!"

"Well," he grunted, "it's a cinch somebody's after you, anyway. I still say it can't be Erlik Khan, because nobody could live after the lick on the head I saw Ali ibn Suleyman hand him, and I don't believe in ghosts. But you've got to be protected until I run down whoever is being so free with his poisoned cigarettes."

"What about yourself? Your name's in his book, too."

"Never mind me," Harrison growled pugnaciously. "I reckon I can take care of myself." He looked capable enough, with his cold blue eyes, and the muscles bulging in his coat. He had shoulders like a bull.

"This wing's practically isolated from the rest of the building," he said, "and you've got the third floor to yourself?"

"Not only the third floor of the wing," she answered. "There's no one else on the third floor anywhere in the building at present."

"That makes it fine!" he exclaimed irritably. "Somebody could sneak in and cut your throat without disturbing anyone. That's what they'll try, too, when they realize the cigarettes didn't finish you. You'd better move to a hotel."

"That wouldn't make any difference," she answered, trembling. Her nerves obviously were in a bad way. "Erlik Khan would find me, anywhere. In a hotel, with people coming and going all the time, and the rotten locks they have on the doors, with transoms and fire escapes and everything, it would just be that much easier for him."

"Well, then, I'll plant a bunch of cops around here."

"That wouldn't do any good, either. Erlik Khan has killed again and again in spite of the police. They do not understand his ways."

"That's right," he muttered uncomfortably aware of a conviction that to summon men from headquarters would surely be signing those men's death warrants, without accomplishing anything else. It was absurd to suppose that the dead Mongol fiend was behind these murderous attacks, yet—Harrison's flesh crawled along his spine at the memory of things that had taken place in River Street—things he had never reported, because he did not wish to be thought either a liar or a madman. The dead do not return—but what seems absurd on Thirty-ninth Boulevard takes on a different aspect among the haunted labyrinths of the Oriental quarter.

"Stay with me!" Joan's eyes were dilated, and she caught Harrison's arm with hands that shook violently. "We can defend these rooms! While one sleeps the other can watch! Do not call the police; their blunders would doom us. You have worked in the quarter for years, and are worth more than the whole police force. The mysterious instincts that are a part of my Eastern heritage are alert to danger. I feel peril for us both, near, creeping closer, gliding around us like serpents in the darkness!"

"But I can't stay here," he scowled worriedly. "We can't barricade ourselves and wait for them to starve us out. I've got to hit back—find out who's behind all this. The best defense is a good offense. But I can't leave you here unguarded, either. Damn!" He clenched his big fists and shook his head like a baffled bull in his perplexity.

"There is one man in the city besides yourself I could trust," she said suddenly. "One worth more than all the police. With him guarding me I could sleep safely."

"Who is he?"

"Khoda Khan."

'That fellow? Why, I thought he'd skipped months ago."

"No; he's been hiding in Levant Street."

"But he's a confounded killer himself!"

"No, he isn't; not according to his standards, which means as much to him as yours do to you. He's an Afghan who was raised in a code of blood-feud and vengeance. He's as honorable according to his creed of life as you or I. And he's my friend. He'd die for me."

"I reckon that means you've been hiding him from the law," said Harrison with a searching glance which she did not seek to evade. He made no further comment. River Street is not South Park Avenue. Harrison's own methods were not always orthodox, but they generally got results.

"Can you reach him?" he asked abruptly. She nodded.

"Alright. Call him and tell him to beat it up here. Tell him he won't be molested by the police, and after the brawl's over, he can go back into hiding. But after that it's open season if I catch him. Use your phone. Wire may be tapped, but we'll have to take the chance. I'll go downstairs and use the booth in the office. Lock the door, and don't open it to anybody until I get back."

When the bolts clicked behind him, Harrison turned down the corridor toward the stairs. The apartment house boasted no elevator. He watched all sides warily as he went. A peculiarity of architecture had, indeed, practically isolated that wing. The wall opposite Joan's doors was blank. The only way to reach the other suites on that floor was to descend the stair and ascend another on the other side of the building.

As he reached the stair he swore softly; his heel had crunched a small vial on the first step. With some vague suspicion of a planted poison trap he stooped and gingerly investigated the splintered bits and the spilled contents. There was a small pool of colorless liquid which gave off a pungent, musky odor, but there seemed nothing lethal about it.

"Some damned Oriental perfume Joan dropped, I reckon," he decided. He descended the twisting stair without further delay and was presently in the booth in the office which opened on the street; a sleepy clerk dozed behind the desk.

Harrison got the chief of police on the wire and began abruptly.

"Say, Hoolihan, you remember that Afghan, Khoda Khan, who knifed a Chinaman about three months ago? Yes, that's the one. Well, listen: I'm using him on a job for a while, so tell your men to lay off, if they see him. Pass the word along *pronto*. Yes, I know it's very irregular; so's the job I hold down. In this case it's the choice of using a fugitive from the law, or seeing a law-abiding citizen murdered. Never mind what it's all about. This is my job, and I've got to handle it my own way. All right; thanks."

He hung up the receiver, thought vigorously for a few minutes, and then dialed another number that was definitely not related to the police station. In place of the chief's booming voice there sounded at the other end of the wire a squeaky whine framed in the argot of the underworld.

"Listen, Johnny," said Harrison with his customary abruptness, "you told me you thought you had a lead on the Kossova murder. What about it?"

"It wasn't no lie, boss!" The voice at the other end trembled with excitement. "I got a tip, and it's big!—*big!* I can't spill it over the phone, and I don't dare stir out. But if you'll meet me at Shan Yang's hop joint, I'll give you the dope. It'll knock you loose from your props, believe me it will!"

"I'll be there in an hour," promised the detective. He left the booth and glanced briefly out into the street. It was a misty night, as so many River Street nights are. Traffic was only a dim echo from some distant, busier section. Drifting fog dimmed the street lamps, shrouding the forms of occasional passers-by. The stage was set for murder; it only awaited the appearance of the actors in the dark drama.

Harrison mounted the stairs again. They wound up out of the office and up into the third story wing without opening upon the second floor at all. The architecture, like much of it in or near the Oriental section, was rather unusual. People of the quarter were notoriously fond of privacy, and even apartment houses were built with this passion in mind. His feet made no sound on the thickly carpeted stairs, though a slight crunching at the top step reminded him of the broken vial again momentarily. He had stepped on the splinters.

He knocked at the locked door, answered Joan's tense challenge and was admitted. He found the girl more self-possessed.

"I talked with Khoda Khan. He's on his way here now. I warned him that the wire might be tapped—that our enemies might know as soon as I called him, and try to stop him on his way here."

"Good," grunted the detective. "While I'm waiting for him I'll have a look at your suite."

There were four rooms, drawing room in front, with a large bedroom behind it, and behind that two smaller rooms, the maid's bedroom and the bathroom. The maid was not there, because Joan had sent her away at the first intimation of danger threatening. The corridor ran parallel with the suite, and the drawing room, large bedroom and bathroom opened upon it. That made three doors to consider. The drawing room had one big east window, overlooking the street, and one on the south. The big bedroom had one south window, and the maid's room one south and one west window. The bathroom had one window, a small one in the west wall, overlooking a small court bounded by a tangle of alleys and board-fenced backyards.

"Three outside doors and six windows to be watched, and this the top story," muttered the detective. "I still think I ought to get some cops here." But he spoke without conviction. He was investigating the bathroom when Joan called him cautiously from the drawing room, telling him that she thought she had heard a faint scratching outside the door. Gun in hand he opened the bathroom door and peered out into the corridor. It was empty. No shape of horror stood before the drawing room door. He closed the door, called reassuringly to the girl, and completed his inspection, grunting approval. Joan La Tour was a daughter of the Oriental quarter. Long ago she had provided against secret enemies as far as special locks and bolts could provide. The windows were guarded with heavy iron-braced shutters, and there was no trapdoor, dumb waiter nor skylight anywhere in the suite.

"Looks like you're ready for a siege," he commented.

"I am. I have canned goods laid away to last for weeks. With Khoda Khan I can hold the fort indefinitely. If things get too hot for you, you'd better come back here yourself—if you can. It's safer than the police station—unless they burn the house down."

A soft rap on the door brought them both around.

"Who is it?" called Joan warily.

"I, Khoda Khan, *sahiba*," came the answer in a low-pitched, but strong and resonant voice. Joan sighed deeply and unlocked the door. A tall figure bowed with a stately gesture and entered.

Khoda Khan was taller than Harrison, and though he lacked something of the American's sheer bulk, his shoulders were equally broad, and his garments could not conceal the hard lines of his limbs, the tigerish suppleness of his motions. His garb was a curious combination of costume, which is common in River Street. He wore a turban which well set off his hawk nose and black beard, and a long silk coat hung nearly to his knees. His trousers were conventional, but a silk sash girdled his lean waist, and his foot-gear was Turkish slippers.

In any costume it would have been equally evident that there was something wild and untamable about the man. His eyes blazed as no civilized man's ever did, and his sinews were like coiled springs under his coat. Harrison felt much as he would have felt if a panther had padded into the room, for the moment placid but ready at an instant's notice to go flying into flaming-eyed, red-taloned action.

"I thought you'd left the country," he said.

The Afghan smiled, a glimmer of white amidst the dark tangle of his beard.

"Nay, *sahib*. That son of a dog I knifed did not die."

"You're lucky he didn't," commented Harrison. "If you kill him you'll hang, sure."

"*Inshallah*," agreed Khoda Khan cheerfully. "But it was a matter of izzat—*honor*. The dog fed me swine's flesh. But no matter. The *memsahib* called me and I came."

"Alright. As long as she needs your protection the police won't arrest you. But when the matter's finished, things stand as they were. I'll give you time to hide again, if you wish, and then I'll try to catch you as I have in the past. Or if you want to surrender and stand trial, I'll promise you as much leniency as possible."

"You speak fairly," answered Khoda Khan. "I will protect the *memsahib*, and when our enemies are dead, you and I will begin our feud anew."

"Do you know anything about these murders?"

"Nay, *sahib*. The *memsahib* called me, saying Mongol dogs threatened her. I came swiftly, over the roofs, lest they seek to ambush me. None molested me. But here is something I found outside the door."

He opened his hand and exhibited a bit of silk, evidently torn from his sash. On it lay a crushed object that Harrison did not recognize. But Joan recoiled with a low cry.

"God! A black scorpion of Assam!"

"Aye—whose sting is death. I saw it running up and down before the door, seeking entrance. Another man might have stepped upon it without seeing it, but I was on my guard, for I smelled the Flower of Death as I came up the stairs. I saw the thing at the door and crushed it before it could sting me."

"What do you mean by the Flower of Death?" demanded Harrison.

"It grows in the jungles where these vermin abide. Its scent attracts them as wine draws a drunkard. A trail of the juice had somehow been laid to this door. Had the door been opened before I slew it, it would have darted in and struck whoever happened to be in its way."

Harrison swore under his breath, remembering the faint scratching noise Joan had heard outside the door.

"I get it now! They put a bottle of that juice on the stairs where it was sure to be stepped on. I did step on it, and broke it, and got the liquid on my shoe. Then I tracked down the stairs, leaving the scent wherever I stepped. Came back upstairs, stepped in the stuff again and tracked it on through the door. Then somebody downstairs turned that scorpion loose—the devil!! That means they've been in this house since I was downstairs!—may be hiding somewhere here now! But somebody had to come into the office to put the scorpion on the trail—I'll ask the clerk—"

"He sleeps like the dead," said Khoda Khan. "He did not waken when I entered and mounted the stairs. What matters if the house is full of Mongols? These doors are strong, and I am alert!" From beneath his coat he drew the terrible Khyber knife—a yard long, with an edge like a razor. "I have slain *men* with this," he announced, grinning like a bearded mountain devil. "Pathans, Indians, a Russian or so. These Mongols are dogs on whom the good steel will be shamed."

"Well," grunted Harrison. "I've got an appointment that's overdue now. I feel queer walking out and leaving you two to fight these devils alone. But there'll be no safety for us until I've smashed this gang at its root, and that's what I'm out to do."

"They'll kill you as you leave the building," said Joan with conviction.

"Well, I've got to risk it. If you're attacked call the police anyway, and call me, at Shan Yang's joint. I'll come back here some time before dawn. But I'm hoping the tip I expect to get will enable me to hit straight at whoever's after us."

He went down the hallway with an eerie feeling of being watched and scanned the stairs as if he expected to see it swarming with black scorpions, and he shied wide of the broken glass on the step. He had an uncomfortable sensation of duty ignored, in spite of himself, though he knew that his two companions did not want the police, and that in dealing with the East it is better to heed the advice of the East.

The clerk still sagged behind his desk. Harrison shook him without avail. The man was not asleep; he was drugged. But his heartbeat was regular, and the detective believed he was in no danger. Anyway, Harrison had no more time to waste. If he kept Johnny Kleck waiting too long, the fellow might become panicky and bolt, to hide in some rat-run for weeks.

He went into the street, where the lamps gleamed luridly through the drifting river mist, half expecting a knife to be thrown at him, or to find a cobra coiled on the seat of his automobile. But he found nothing his suspicion anticipated, even though he lifted the hood and the rumble-seat to see if a bomb had been planted. Satisfying himself at last, he climbed in and the girl watching him through the slits of a third-story shutter sighed relievedly to see him roar away unmolested.

Khoda Khan had gone through the rooms, giving approval in his beard of the locks, and having extinguished the lights in the other chambers he returned to the drawing room, where he turned out all lights there except one small desk lamp. It shed a pool of light in the center of the room, leaving the rest in shadowy vagueness.

"Darkness baffles rogues as well as honest men," he said sagely, "and I see like a cat in the dark."

He sat cross-legged near the door that let into the bedroom, which he left partly open. He merged with the shadows so that all of him Joan could make out with any distinctness was his turban and the glimmer of his eyes as he turned his head.

"We will remain in this room, *sahiba,*" he said. "Having failed with poison and reptile, it is certain that men will next be sent. Lie down on that divan and sleep, if you can. I will keep watch."

Joan obeyed, but she did not sleep. Her nerves seemed to thrum with tautness. The silence of the house oppressed her, and the few noises of the street made her start.

Khoda Khan sat motionless as a statue, imbued with the savage patience and immobility of the hills that bred him. Grown to manhood on the raw barbaric edge of the world, where survival depended on personal ability, his senses were whetted keener than is possible for civilized men. Even Harrison's trained faculties were blunt in comparison. Khoda Khan could still smell the faint aroma of the Flower of Death, mingled with the acrid odor of the crushed scorpion. He heard and identified every sound in or outside the house—knew which were natural, and which were not.

He heard the sounds on the roof long before his warning hiss brought Joan upright on the divan. The Afghan's eyes glowed like phosphorus in the shadows and his teeth glimmered dimly in a savage grin. Joan looked at him inquiringly. Her civilized ears heard nothing. But he heard and with his ears followed the sounds accurately and located the place where they halted. Joan heard something then, a faint scratching somewhere in the building, but she did not identify it—as Khoda Khan did—as the forcing of the shutters on the bathroom window.

With a quick reassuring gesture to her, Khoda Khan rose and melted like a slinking leopard into the darkness of the bedroom. She took up a blunt-nosed automatic, with no great conviction of reliance upon it, and groped on the table for a bottle of wine, feeling an intense need of stimulants. She was shaking in every limb and cold sweat was gathering on her flesh. She remembered the cigarettes, but the unbroken seal on the bottle reassured her. Even the wisest have their thoughtless moments. It was not until she had begun to drink that the peculiar flavor made her realize that the man who had shifted the cigarettes might just as easily have taken a bottle of wine and left another in its place, a facsimile that included an unbroken seal. She fell back on the divan, gagging.

Khoda Khan wasted no time, because he heard other sounds, out in the hall. His ears told him, as he crouched by the bathroom door, that the shutters had been forced—done almost in silence, a job that a white man would have made sound like an explosion in an iron foundry—and now the window was being jimmied. Then he heard something stealthy and bulky drop into the room. Then it was that he threw open the door and charged in like a typhoon, his long knife held low.

Enough light filtered into the room from outside to limn a powerful, crouching figure, with dim snarling yellow features. The intruder yelped explosively, started a motion—and then the long Khyber knife, driven by an arm nerved to the fury of the Himalayas, ripped him open from groin to breastbone.

Khoda Khan did not pause. He knew there was only one man in the room, but through the open window he saw a thick rope dangling from above. He sprang forward, grasped it with both hands and heaved backward like a bull. The men on the roof holding it released it to keep from being jerked headlong over the edge, and he tumbled backward, sprawling over the corpse, the loose rope in his hands. He yelped exultantly, then sprang up and glided to the door that opened into the corridor. Unless they had another rope, which was unlikely, the men on the roof were temporarily out of the fight.

He flung open the door and ducked deeply. A hatchet cut a great chip out the jamb, and he stabbed upward once, then sprang over a writhing body into the corridor, jerking a big pistol from its hidden scabbard.

The bright light of the corridor did not blind him. He saw a second hatchet-man crouching by the bedroom door, and a man in the silk robes of a mandarin working at the lock of the drawing room door. He was between them and the stairs. As they wheeled toward him he shot the hatchet-man in the belly. An automatic spat in the hand of the mandarin, and Khoda Khan felt the wind of the bullet. The next instant his own gun roared again and the Manchu staggered, the pistol flying from a hand that was suddenly a dripping red pulp. Then he whipped a long knife from his robes with his left hand and came along the corridor like a hurricane, his eyes glaring and his silk garments whipping about him.

Khoda Khan shot him through the head and the mandarin fell so near his feet that the long knife stuck into the floor and quivered a matter of inches from the Afghan's slipper.

But Khoda Khan paused only long enough to pass his knife through the hatchet-man he had shot in the belly—for his fighting ethics were those of the savage Hills—and then he turned and ran back into the bathroom. He fired a shot through the window, though the men on the roof were making further demonstration, and then ran through the bedroom, snapping on lights as he went.

"I have slain the dogs, *sahiba*!" he exclaimed. "By Allah, they have tasted lead and steel! Others are on the roof but they are helpless for the moment. But men will come to investigate the shots, that being the custom of the *sahibs*, so it is expedient that we decide on our further actions, and the proper lies to tell—Allah!"

Joan La Tour stood bolt upright, clutching the back of the divan. Her face was the color of marble, and the expression was rigid too, like a mask of horror carved in stone. Her dilated eyes blazed like weird black fire.

"Allah shield us against Shaitan the Damned!" ejaculated Khoda Khan, making a sign with his fingers that antedated Islam by some thousands of years. "What has happened to you, *sahiba*?"

He moved toward her, to be met by a scream that sent him cowering back, cold sweat starting out on his flesh.

"Keep back!" she cried in a voice he did not recognize. "You are a demon! You are all demons! I see you! I hear your cloven feet padding in the night! I see your eyes blazing from the shadows! Keep your taloned hands from me! *Aie!*" Foam flecked her lips as she screamed blasphemies in English and Arabic that made Khoda Khan's hair stand stiffly on end.

"*Sahiba!*" he begged, trembling like a leaf. "I am no demon! I am Khoda Khan! I—" His outstretched hand touched her, and with an awful shriek she turned and darted for the door, tearing at the bolts. He sprang to stop her, but in her frenzy she was even quicker than he. She whipped the door open, eluded his grasping hand and flew down the corridor, deaf to his anguished yells.

When Harrison left Joan's house, he drove straight to Shan Yang's dive, which, in the heart of River Street, masqueraded as a low-grade drinking joint. It was late. Only a few derelicts huddled about the bar, and he noticed that the barman was a Chinaman that he had never seen before. He stared impassively at Harrison, but jerked a thumb toward the back door, masked by dingy curtains, when the detective asked abruptly: "Johnny Kleck here?"

Harrison passed through the door, traversed a short dimly-lighted hallway and rapped authoritatively on the door at the other end. In the silence he heard rats scampering. A steel disk in the center of the door shifted and a slanted black eye glittered in the opening.

"Open the door, Shan Yang," ordered Harrison impatiently, and the eye was withdrawn, accompanied by the rattling of bolts and chains.

He pushed open the door and entered the room whose illumination was scarcely better than that of the corridor. It was a large, dingy, drab affair, lined with bunks. Fires sputtered in braziers, and Shan Yang was making his way to his accustomed seat behind a low counter near the wall. Harrison spent but a single casual glance on the familiar figure, the well-known dingy silk jacket worked in gilt dragons. Then he strode across the room to a door in the wall opposite the counter to which Shan Yang was making his way. This was an opium joint and Harrison knew it—knew those figures in the bunks were Chinamen sleeping the sleep of the smoke. Why he had not raided it, as he had raided and destroyed other opium-dens, only Harrison could have said. But law-enforcement on River Street is not the orthodox routine it is on Baskerville Avenue, for instance. Harrison's reasons were those of expediency and necessity. Sometimes certain conventions have to be sacrificed for the sake of more important gains—especially when the law-enforcement of a whole district (and in the Oriental quarter) rests on one's shoulders.

A characteristic smell pervaded the dense atmosphere, in spite of the reek of dope and unwashed bodies—the dank odor of the river, which hangs over the River Street dives or wells up from their floors like the black intangible spirit of the quarter itself. Shan Yang's dive, like many others, was built on the very bank of the river. The back room projected out over the water on rotting piles, at which the black river lapped hungrily.

Harrison opened the door, entered and pushed it to behind him, his lips framing a greeting that was never uttered. He stood dumbly, glaring.

He was in a small dingy room, bare except for a crude table and some chairs. An oil lamp on the table cast a smoky light. And in that light he saw Johnny Kleck. The man stood bolt upright against the far wall, his arms spread like a crucifix, rigid, his eyes glassy and staring, his mean, ratty features twisted in a frozen grin. He did not speak, and Harrison's gaze, traveling down him, halted with a shock. Johnny's feet did not touch the floor by several inches—

Harrison's big blue pistol jumped into his hand. Johnny Kleck was dead, that grin was a contortion of horror and agony. He was crucified to the wall by skewer-like dagger blades through his wrists and ankles, his ears spiked to the wall to keep his head upright. But that was not what had killed him. The bosom of Johnny's shirt was charred, and there was a round, blackened hole.

Feeling suddenly sick the detective wheeled, opened the door and stepped back into the larger room. The light seemed dimmer, the smoke thicker than ever. No mumblings came from the bunks; the fires in the braziers burned blue, with weird sputterings. Shan Yang crouched behind the counter. His shoulders moved as if he were tallying beads on an abacus.

"Shan Yang!" the detective's voice grated harshly in the murky silence. "Who's been in that room tonight besides Johnny Kleck?"

The man behind the counter straightened and looked full at him, and Harrison felt his skin crawl. Above the gilt-worked jacket an unfamiliar face returned his gaze. That was no Shan Yang; it was a man he had never seen—it was a Mongol. He started and stared about him as the men in the bunks rose with supple ease. They were not Chinese; they were Mongols to a man, and their slanted black eyes were not clouded by drugs.

With a curse Harrison sprang toward the outer door and with a rush they were on him. His gun crashed and a man staggered in mid-stride. Then the lights went out, the braziers were overturned, and in the stygian blackness hard bodies caromed against the detective. Long-nailed fingers clawed at his throat, thick arms locked about his waist and legs. Somewhere a sibilant voice was hissing orders.

Harrison's mauling left worked like a piston, crushing flesh and bone; his right wielded the gun barrel like a club. He forged toward the unseen door blindly, dragging his assailants by sheer strength. He seemed to be wading through a solid mass, as if the darkness had turned to bone and muscle about him. A knife licked through his coat, stinging his skin, and then he gasped as a silk cord looped about his neck, shutting off his wind, sinking deeper and deeper into the straining flesh. Blindly he jammed the muzzle against the nearest body and pulled the trigger. At the muffled concussion something fell away from him and the strangling agony lessened. Gasping for breath he groped and tore the cord away—then he was borne down under a rush of heavy bodies and something smashed savagely against his head. The darkness exploded in a shower of sparks that were instantly quenched in stygian blackness.

*   *   *

The smell of the river was in Steve Harrison's nostrils as he re-
gained his addled senses, river-scent mingled with the odor of stale
blood. The blood, he realized, when he had enough sense to realize
anything, was clotted on his own scalp. His head swam and he tried to
raise a hand to it, thereby discovering that he was bound hand and
foot with cords that cut into the flesh. A candle was dazzling his eyes,
and for awhile he could see nothing else. Then things began to assume
their proper proportions, and objects grew out of nothing and became
identifiable.

He was lying on a bare floor of new, unpainted wood, in a large
square chamber, the walls of which were of stone, without paint or
plaster. The ceiling was likewise of stone, with heavy, bare beams, and
there was an open trap door almost directly above him, through
which, in spite of the candle, he got a glimpse of stars. Fresh air flowed
through that trap, bearing with it the river-smell stronger than ever.
The chamber was bare of furniture, the candle stuck in a niche in the
wall. Harrison swore, wondering if he was delirious. This was like an
experience in a dream, with everything unreal and distorted.

He tried to struggle to a sitting position, but that made his head
swim, so that he lay back and swore fervently. He yelled wrathfully,
and a face peered down at him through the trap—a square, yellow face
with beady slanted eyes. He cursed the face and it mocked him and
was withdrawn. The noise of the door softly opening checked Harrison's profanity and he wriggled around to glare at the intruder.

And he glared in silence, feeling an icy prickling up and down his
spine. Once before he had lain bound and helpless, staring up at a tall
black-robed figure whose yellow eyes glimmered from the shadow of a
dusky hood. But that man was dead; Harrison had seen him cut down
by the scimitar of a maddened Druse.

"Erlik Khan!" The words were forced out of him. He licked lips suddenly dry.

"*Aie!*" It was the same ghostly, hollow voice that had chilled him in the old days. "Erlik Khan, the Lord of the Dead."

"Are you a man or a ghost?" demanded Harrison.

"I live."

"But I saw Ali ibn Suleyman kill you!" exclaimed the detective. "He slashed you across the head with a heavy sword that was sharp as a razor. He was a stronger man than I am. He struck with the full power of his arm. Your hood fell in two pieces—"

"And I fell like a dead man in my own blood," finished Erlik Khan. "But the steel cap I wore—as I wear now—under my hood, saved my life as it has more than once. The terrible stroke cracked it across the top and cut my scalp, fracturing my skull and causing concussion of the brain. But I lived, and some of my faithful followers, who escaped the sword of the Druse, carried me down through the subterranean tunnels which led from my house, and so I escaped the burning building. But I lay like a dead man for weeks, and it was not until a very wise man was brought from Mongolia that I recovered my senses, and sanity.

"But now I am ready to take up my work where I left off, though I must rebuild much. Many of my former followers had forgotten my authority. Some required to be taught anew who was master."

"And you've been teaching them," grunted Harrison, recovering his pugnacious composure.

"True. Some examples had to be made. One man fell from a roof, a snake bit another, yet another ran into knives in a dark alley. Then there was another matter. Joan La Tour betrayed me in the old days. She knows too many secrets. She had to die. So that she might taste agony in anticipation, I sent her a page from my book of the dead."

"Your devils killed Kleck," accused Harrison.

"Of course. All wires leading from the girl's apartment house are tapped. I myself heard your conversation with Kleck. That is why you were not attacked when you left the building. I saw that you were playing into my hands. I sent my men to take possession of Shan Yang's dive. He had no more use for his jacket, presently, so one donned it to deceive you. Kleck had somehow learned of my return; these stool pigeons are clever. But he had time to regret. A man dies hard with a white-hot point of iron bored through his breast."

Harrison said nothing and presently the Mongol continued.

"I wrote your name in my book because I recognized you as my most dangerous opponent. It was because of you that Ali ibn Suleyman turned against me.

"I am rebuilding my empire again, but more solidly. First I shall consolidate River Street, and create a political machine to rule the city. The men in office now do not suspect my existence. If all were to die, it would not be hard to find others to fill their places—men who are not indifferent to the clink of gold."

"You're mad," growled Harrison. "Control a whole city government from a dive in River Street?"

"It has been done," answered the Mongol tranquilly. "I will strike like a cobra from the dark. Only the men who obey my agent will live. He will be a white man, a figurehead whom men will think the real power, while I remain unseen. You might have been he, if you had a little more intelligence."

He took a bulky object from under his arm, a thick book with glossy black covers—ebony with green jade hinges. He riffled the night-hued pages and Harrison saw they were covered with crimson characters.

"My book of the dead," said Erlik Khan. "Many names have been crossed out. Many more have been added since I recovered my sanity.

Some of them would interest you; they include names of the mayor, the chief of police, district attorney, a number of aldermen."

"That lick must have addled your brains permanently," snarled Harrison. "Do you think you can substitute a whole city government and get away with it?"

"I can and will. These men will die in various ways, and men of my own choice will succeed them in office. Within a year I will hold this city in the palm of my hand, and there will be none to interfere with me."

Lying staring up at the bizarre figure, whose features were, as always, shadowed beyond recognition by the hood, Harrison's flesh crawled with the conviction that the Mongol was indeed mad. His crimson dreams, always ghastly, were too grotesque and incredible for the visions of a wholly sane man. Yet he was dangerous as a maddened cobra. His monstrous plot must ultimately fail, yet he held the lives of many men in his hand. And Harrison, on whom the city relied for protection from whatever menace the Oriental quarter might spawn, lay bound and helpless before him. The detective cursed in fury.

"Always the man of violence," mocked Erlik Khan, with the suggestion of scorn in his voice. "Barbarian! Who lays his trust in guns and blades, who would check the stride of imperial power with blows of the naked fists! Brainless arm striking blind blows! Well, you have struck your last. Smell the river damp that creeps in through the ceiling? Soon it shall enfold you utterly and your dreams and aspirations will be one with the mist of the river."

"Where are we?" demanded Harrison.

"On an island below the city, where the marshes begin. Once there were warehouses here, and a factory, but they were abandoned as the city grew in the other direction, and have been crumbling into ruin for twenty years. I purchased the entire island through one of my agents, and am rebuilding to suit my own purposes an old stone man-sion which stood here before the factory was built. None notices, be-cause my own henchmen are the workmen, and no one ever comes to this marshy island. The house is invisible from the river, hidden as it is among the tangle of old rotting warehouses. You came here in a mo-torboat which was anchored beneath the rotting wharves behind Shan Yang's dive. Another boat will presently fetch my men who were sent to dispose of Joan La Tour."

'They may not find that so easy," commented the detective.

"Never fear. I know she summoned that hairy wolf, Khoda Khan, to her aid, and it's true that my men failed to slay him before he reached her. But I suppose it was a false sense of trust in the Afghan that caused you to make your appointment with Kleck. I rather ex-pected you to remain with the foolish girl and try to protect her in your way."

Somewhere below them a gong sounded. Erlik Khan did not start, but there was a surprise in the lift of his head. He closed the black book.

"I have wasted enough time on you," he said. "Once before I bade you farewell in one of my dungeons. Then the fanaticism of a crazy Druse saved you. This time there will be no upset of my plans. The only men in this house are Mongols, who know no law but my will. I go, but you will not be lonely. Soon one will come to you."

And with a low, chilling laugh the phantom-like figure moved through the door and disappeared. Outside a lock clicked, and then there was stillness.

The silence was broken suddenly by a muffled scream. It came from somewhere below and was repeated half a dozen times. Harrison shuddered. No one who has ever visited an insane asylum could fail to recognize that sound. It was the shrieking of a mad woman. After these cries the silence seemed even more stifling and menacing.

Harrison swore to quiet his feelings, and again the velvet-capped head of the Mongol leered down at him through the trap.

"Grin, you yellow-bellied ape!" roared Harrison, tugging at his cords until the veins stood out on his temples. "If I could break these damned ropes I'd knock that grin around where your pigtail ought to be, you—" He went into minute details of the Mongol's ancestry, dwelling at length on the more scandalous phases of it, and in the midst of his noisy tirade he saw the leer change suddenly to a startled snarl. The head vanished from the trap and there came a sound like the blow of a butcher's cleaver.

Then another face was poked into the trap—a wild, bearded face, with blazing, bloodshot eyes, and surmounted by a disheveled turban.

"Sahib!" hissed the apparition.

"Khoda Khan!" ejaculated the detective, galvanized. "What the devil are you doing here?"

"Softly!" muttered the Afghan. "Let not the accursed ones hear!"

He tossed the loose end of a rope ladder down through the trap and came down in a rush, his bare feet making no sound as he hit the floor. He held his long knife in his teeth, and blood dripped from the point.

Squatting beside the detective he cut him free with reckless slashes that threatened to slice flesh as well as hemp. The Afghan was quivering with half-controlled passion. His teeth gleamed like a wolf's fangs amidst the tangle of his beard.

Harrison sat up, chafing his swollen wrists.

"Where's Joan? Quick, man, where is she?"

"Here! In this accursed den!"

"But—"

"That was she screaming a few minutes ago," broke in the Afghan, and Harrison's flesh crawled with a vague monstrous premonition.

"But that was a mad woman!" he almost whispered.

"The *sahiba* is mad," said Khoda Khan somberly. "Hearken, *sahib*, and then judge if the fault is altogether mine.

"After you left, the accursed ones let down a man from the roof on a rope. Him I knifed, and I slew three more who sought to force the doors. But when I returned to the *sahiba*, she knew me not. She fled from me into the street, and other devils must have been lurking nearby, because as she ran shrieking along the sidewalk, a big automobile loomed out of the fog and a Mongol stretched forth an arm and dragged her into the car, from under my very fingers. I saw his accursed yellow face by the light of a street lamp.

"Knowing she were better dead by a bullet than in their hands, I emptied my pistol after the car, but it fled like Shaitan the Damned from the face of Allah, and if I hit anyone in it, I know not. Then as I rent my garments and cursed the day of my birth—for I could not pursue it on foot—Allah willed that another automobile should appear. It was driven by a young man in evening clothes, returning from a revel, no doubt, and being cursed with curiosity he slowed down near the curb to observe my grief.

"So, praising Allah, I sprang in beside him and placing my knife point against his ribs bade him go with speed and he obeyed in great fear. The car of the damned ones was out of sight, but presently I glimpsed it again, and exhorted the youth to greater speed, so the machine seemed to fly like the steed of the Prophet. So, presently I saw the car halt at the river bank. I made the youth halt likewise, and he sprang out and fled in the other direction in terror.

"I ran through the darkness, hot for the blood of the accursed ones, but before I could reach the bank I saw four Mongols leave the car, carrying the *memsahib* who was bound and gagged, and they entered a motorboat and headed out into the river toward an island which lay on the breast of the water like a dark cloud.

"I cast up and down on the shore like a madman, and was about to leap in and swim, though the distance was great, when I came upon a boat chained to a pile, but one driven by oars. I gave praise to Allah and cut the chain with my knife—see the nick in the edge?—and rowed after the accursed ones with great speed.

"They were far ahead of me, but Allah willed it that their engine should sputter and cease when they had almost reached the island. So I took heart, hearing them cursing in their heathen tongue, and hoped to draw alongside and slay them all before they were aware of me. They saw me not in the darkness, nor heard my oars because of their own noises, but before I could reach them the accursed engine began again. So they reached a wharf on the marshy shore ahead of me, but they lingered to make the boat fast, so I was not too far behind them as they bore the *memsahib* through the shadows of the crumbling shacks which stood all about.

"Then I was hot to overtake and slay them, but before I could come up with them they had reached the door of a great stone house—this one, *sahib*—set in a tangle of rotting buildings. A steel fence surrounded it, with razor-edged spearheads set along the top but by Allah, that could not hinder a *lifter* of the Khyber! I went over it without so much as tearing my garments. Inside was a second wall of stone, but it stood in ruins.

"I crouched in the shadows near the house and saw that the windows were heavily barred and the doors strong. Moreover, the lower part of the house is full of armed men. So I climbed a corner of the wall, and it was not easy, but presently I reached the roof which at that part is flat, with a parapet. I expected a watcher, and so there was, but he was too busy taunting his captive to see or hear me until my knife sent him to Hell. Here is his dagger; he bore no gun."

Harrison mechanically took the wicked, lean-bladed poniard.

"But what caused Joan to go mad?"

"*Sahib,* there was a broken wine bottle on the floor, and a goblet. I had no time to investigate it, but I know that wine must have been poisoned with the juice of the fruit called the black pomegranate. She can not have drunk much, or she would have died frothing and champing like a mad dog. But only a little will rob one of sanity. It grows in the jungles of Indo-China, and white men say it is a lie. But it is no lie; thrice I have seen men die after having drunk its juice, and more than once I have seen men, and women too, turn mad because of it. I have traveled in that hellish country where it grows."

"God!" Harrison's foundations were shaken by nausea. Then his big hands clenched into chunks of iron and baleful fire glimmered in his savage blue eyes. The weakness of horror and revulsion was followed by cold fury dangerous as the blood-hunger of a timber wolf.

"She may be already dead," he muttered thickly. "But dead or alive we'll send Erlik Khan to Hell. Try that door."

It was of heavy teak, braced with bronze straps.

"It is locked," muttered the Afghan. "We will burst it."

He was about to launch his shoulder against it when he stopped short, the long Khyber knife jumping into his fist like a beam of light.

"Someone approaches!" he whispered, and a second later Harrison's more civilized—and therefore duller—ears caught a cat-like tread.

Instantly he acted. He shoved the Afghan behind the door and sat down quickly in the center of the room, wrapped a piece of rope about his ankles and then lay full length, his arms behind and under him. He was lying on the other pieces of severed cord, concealing them, and to the casual glance he resembled a man lying bound hand and foot. The Afghan understood and grinned hugely.

Harrison worked with the celerity of trained mind and muscles that eliminates fumbling delay and bungling. He accomplished his purpose in a matter of seconds and without undue noise. A key grated in the lock as he settled himself, and then the door swung open. A giant Mongol stood limned in the opening. His head was shaven, his square features passionless as the face of a copper idol. In one hand he carried a curiously shaped ebony block, in the other a mace such as was borne by the horsemen of Ghengis Khan—a straight-hafted iron bludgeon with a round head covered with steel points, and a knob on the other end to keep the hand from slipping.

He did not see Khoda Khan because when he threw back the door, the Afghan was hidden behind it. Khoda Khan did not stab him as he entered because the Afghan could not see into the outer corridor, and had no way of knowing how many men were following the first. But the Mongol was alone, and he did not bother to shut the door. He went straight to the man lying on the floor, scowling slightly to see the rope ladder hanging down through the trap, as if it was not usual to leave it that way, but he did not show any suspicion or call to the man on the roof.

He did not examine Harrison's cords. The detective presented the appearance the Mongol had expected, and this fact blunted his faculties as anything taken for granted is likely to do. As he bent down, over his shoulder Harrison saw Khoda Khan glide from behind the door as silently as a panther.

Leaning his mace against his leg, spiked head on the floor, the Mongol grasped Harrison's shirt bosom with one hand, lifted his head and shoulders clear of the floor, while he shoved the block under his head. Like twin striking snakes the detective's hands whipped from behind him and locked on the Mongol's bull throat.

There was no cry; instantly the Mongol's slant eyes distended and his lips parted in a grin of strangulation. With a terrific heave he reared upright, dragging Harrison with him, but not breaking his hold, and the weight of the big American pulled them both down again. Both yellow hands tore frantically at Harrison's iron wrists; then the giant stiffened convulsively and brief agony reddened his black eyes. Khoda Khan had driven his knife between the Mongol's shoulders so that the point cut through the silk over the man's breastbone.

Harrison caught up the mace, grunting with savage satisfaction. It was a weapon more suited to his temperament than the dagger Khoda Khan had given him. No need to ask its use; if he had been bound and alone when the executioner entered, his brains would now have been clotting its spiked ball and the hollowed ebon block which so nicely accommodated a human head. Erlik Khan's executions varied along the whole gamut from the exquisitely subtle to the crudely bestial.

"The door's open," said Harrison. "Let's go!"

There were no keys on the body. Harrison doubted if the key in the door would fit any other in the building, but he locked the door and pocketed the key, hoping that would prevent the body from being soon discovered.

They emerged into a dim-lit corridor which presented the same unfinished appearance as the room they had just left. At the other end stairs wound down into shadowy gloom, and they descended warily, Harrison feeling along the wall to guide his steps. Khoda Khan seemed to see like a cat in the dark; he went down silently and surely. But it was Harrison who discovered the door. His hand, moving along the convex surface, felt the smooth stone give way to wood—a short narrow panel, through which a man could just squeeze. When the wall was covered with tapestry—as he knew it would be when Erlik Khan completed his house—it would be sufficiently hidden for a secret entrance.

Khoda Khan, behind him, was growing impatient at the delay, when somewhere below them both heard a noise simultaneously. It might have been a man ascending the winding stairs and it might not, but Harrison acted instinctively. He pushed and the door opened inward on noiseless oiled springs. A groping foot discovered narrow steps inside. With a whispered word to the Afghan he stepped through and Khoda Khan followed. He pulled the door shut again and they stood in total blackness with a curving wall on either hand. Harrison struck a match and a narrow stairs was revealed, winding down.

"This place must be built like a castle," Harrison muttered, wondering at the thickness of the walls. The match went out and they groped down in darkness too thick for even the Afghan to pierce. And suddenly both halted in their tracks. Harrison estimated that they had reached the level of the second floor, and through the inner wall came the mutter of voices. Harrison groped for another door, or a peep-hole for spying, but he found nothing of the sort. But straining his ear close to the stone, he began to understand what was being said beyond the wall, and a long-drawn hiss between clenched teeth told him that Khoda Khan likewise understood.

The first voice was Erlik Khan's; there was no mistaking that hollow reverberance. It was answered by a piteous, incoherent whimpering that brought sweat suddenly out on Harrison's flesh.

"No," the Mongol was saying. "I have come back, not from Hell as your barbarian superstitions suggest, but from a refuge unknown to your stupid police. I was saved from death by the steel cap I always wear beneath my coif. You are at a loss as to how you got here?"

"I don't understand!" It was the voice of Joan La Tour, half-hysterical, but undeniably sane. "I remember opening a bottle of wine, and as soon as I drank I knew it was drugged. Then everything faded out—I don't remember anything except great black walls, and awful shapes skulking in the darkness. I ran through gigantic shadowy halls for a thousand years—"

"They were hallucinations of madness, of the juice of the black pomegranate," answered Erlik Khan. Khoda Khan was muttering blasphemously in his beard until Harrison admonished him to silence with a fierce dig of his elbow. "If you had drunk more you would have died like a rabid dog. As it was, you went insane. But I knew the antidote—possessed the drug that restored your sanity."

"Why?" the girl whimpered bewilderedly.

"Because I did not wish you to die like a candle blown out in the dark, my beautiful white orchid. I wish you to be fully sane so as to taste to the last dregs the shame and agony of death, subtle and prolonged. For the exquisite, an exquisite death. For the coarse-fibered, the death of an ox, such as I have decreed for your friend Harrison."

"That will be more easily decreed than executed," she retorted with a flash of spirit.

"It is already accomplished," the Mongol asserted imperturbably. "The executioner has gone to him, and by this time Mr. Harrison's head resembles a crushed egg."

"Oh, God!" At the sick grief and pain in that moan Harrison winced and fought a frantic desire to shout out denial and reassurance.

Then she remembered something else to torture her.

"Khoda Khan! What have you done with Khoda Khan?"

The Afghan's fingers clamped like iron on Harrison's arm at the sound of his name.

"When my men brought you away they did not take time to deal with him," replied the Mongol. "They had not expected to take you alive, and when fate cast you into their hands, they came away in haste. He matters little. True, he killed four of my best men, but that was merely the deed of a wolf. He has no mentality. He and the detective are much alike—mere masses of brawn, brainless, helpless against intellect like mine. Presently I shall attend to him. His corpse shall be thrown on a dung-heap with a dead pig."

"Allah!" Harrison felt Khoda Khan trembling with fury. "Liar! I will feed his yellow guts to the rats!"

Only Harrison's grip on his arm kept the maddened Moslem from attacking the stone wall in an effort to burst through to his enemy. The detective was running his hand over the surface, seeking a door, but only blank stone rewarded him. Erlik Khan had not had time to provide his unfinished house with as many secrets as his rat-runs usually possessed.

They heard the Mongol clap his hands authoritatively, and they sensed the entrance of men into the room. Staccato commands followed in Mongolian, there was a sharp cry of pain or fear, and then silence followed the soft closing of a door. Though they could not see, both men knew instinctively that the chamber on the other side of the wall was empty. Harrison almost strangled with a panic of helpless rage. He was penned in these infernal walls and Joan La Tour was being borne away to some abominable doom.

"*Wallah!*" the Afghan was raving. "They have taken her away to slay her! Her life and our *izzat* is at stake! By the Prophet's beard and my feet! I will burn this accursed house! I will slake the fire with Mongol blood! In Allah's name, *sahib*, let us do something!"

"Come on!" snarled Harrison. "There must be another door somewhere!"

Recklessly they plunged down the winding stair, and about the time they had reached the first floor level, Harrison's groping hand felt a door. Even as he found the catch, it moved under his fingers. Their noise must have been heard through the wall, for the panel opened, and a shaven head was poked in, framed in the square of light. The Mongol blinked in the darkness, and Harrison brought the mace down on his head, experiencing a vengeful satisfaction as he felt the skull give way beneath the iron spikes. The man fell face down in the narrow opening and Harrison sprang over his body into the outer room before he took time to learn if there were others. But the chamber was untenanted. It was thickly carpeted, the walls hung with black velvet tapestries. The doors were of bronze-bound teak, with gilt-worked arches. Khoda Khan presented an incongruous contrast, barefooted, with draggled turban and red-smeared knife.

But Harrison did not pause to philosophize. Ignorant as he was of the house, one way was as good as another. He chose a door at random and flung it open, revealing a wide corridor carpeted and tapestried like the chamber. At the other end, through wide satin curtains that hung from roof to floor, a file of men was just disappearing—tall, black-silk clad Mongols, heads bent somberly, like a train of dusky ghosts. They did not look back.

"Follow them!" snapped Harrison. "They must be headed for the execution—"

Khoda Khan was already sweeping down the corridor like a vengeful whirlwind. The thick carpet deadened their footfalls, so even Harrison's big shoes made no noise. There was a distinct feeling of unreality, running silently down that fantastic hall—it was like a dream in which natural laws are suspended. Even in that moment Harrison had time to reflect that this whole night had been like a nightmare, possible only in the Oriental quarter, its violence and bloodshed like an evil dream. Erlik Khan had loosed the forces of chaos and insanity; murder had gone mad, and its frenzy was imparted to all actions and men caught in its maelstrom.

Khoda Khan would have burst headlong through the curtains—he was already drawing breath for a yell, and lifting his knife—if Harrison had not seized him. The Afghan's sinews were like cords under the detective's hands, and Harrison doubted his own ability to restrain him forcibly, but a vestige of sanity remained to the hillman.

Pushing him back, Harrison gazed between the curtains. There was a great double-valved door there, but it was partly open, and he looked into the room beyond. Khoda Khan's beard was jammed hard against his neck as the Afghan glared over his shoulder.

It was a large chamber, hung like the others with black velvet on which golden dragons writhed. There were thick rugs, and lanterns hanging from the ivory-inlaid ceiling cast a red glow that made for illusion. Black-robed men ranged along the wall might have been shadows but for their glittering eyes.

On a throne-like chair of ebony sat a grim figure, motionless as an image except when its loose robes stirred in the faintly moving air. Harrison felt the short hairs prickle at the back of his neck, just as a dog's hackles rise at the sight of an enemy. Khoda Khan muttered some incoherent blasphemy.

The Mongol's throne was set against a side wall. No one stood near him as he sat in solitary magnificence, like an idol brooding on human doom. In the center of the room stood what looked uncomfortably like a sacrificial altar—a curiously carved block of stone that might have come out of the heart of the Gobi. On that stone lay Joan La Tour, white as a marble statue, her arms outstretched like a crucifix, her hands and feet extending over the edges of the block. Her dilated eyes stared upward as one lost to hope, aware of doom and eager only for death to put an end to agony. The physical torture had not yet begun, but a gaunt half-naked brute squatted on his haunches at the end of the altar, heating the point of a bronze rod in a dish full of glowing coals.

"Damn!" It was half curse, half sob of fury bursting from Harrison's lips. Then he was hurled aside and Khoda Khan burst into the room like a flying dervish, bristling beard, blazing eyes, knife and all. Erlik Khan came erect with a startled guttural as the Afghan came tearing down the room like a headlong hurricane of destruction. The torturer sprang up just in time to meet the yard-long knife lashing down, and it split his skull down through the teeth.

"*Aie!*" It was a howl from a score of Mongol throats.

"*Allaho akabar!*" yelled Khoda Khan, whirling the red knife about his head. He threw himself on the altar, slashing at Joan's bonds with a frenzy that threatened to dismember the girl.

Then from all sides the black-robed figures swarmed in, not noticing in their confusion that the Afghan had been followed by another grim figure who came with less abandon but with equal ferocity.

They were aware of Harrison only when he dealt a prodigious sweep of his mace, right and left, bowling men over like ten-pins, and reached the altar through the gap made in the bewildered throng. Khoda Khan had freed the girl and he wheeled, spitting like a cat, his bared teeth gleaming and each hair of his beard stiffly on end.

"*Allah!*" he yelled—spat in the faces of the oncoming Mongols—crouched as if to spring into the midst of them—then whirled and rushed headlong at the ebony throne.

The speed and unexpectedness of the move were stunning. With a choked cry Erlik Khan fired and missed at point-blank range—and then the breath burst from Khoda Khan in an ear-splitting yell as his knife plunged into the Mongol's breast and the point sprang a hand's breadth out of his black-clad back.

The impetus of his rush unchecked, Khoda Khan hurtled into the falling figure, crashing it back onto the ebony throne which splintered under the impact of the two heavy bodies. Bounding up, wrenching his dripping knife free, Khoda Khan whirled it high and howled like a wolf.

"*Ya Allah!* Wearer of steel caps! Carry the taste of my knife in your guts to Hell with you!"

There was a long hissing intake of breath as the Mongols stared wide-eyed at the black-robed, red-smeared figure crumpled grotesquely among the ruins of the broken throne; and in the instant that they stood like frozen men, Harrison caught up Joan and ran for the nearest door, bellowing: "Khoda Khan! This way! Quick!"

With a howl and a whickering of blades the Mongols were at his heels. Fear of steel in his back winged Harrison's big feet, and Khoda Khan ran slantingly across the room to meet him at the door.

"Haste, *sahib*! Down the corridor! I will cover you retreat!"

"No! Take Joan and run!" Harrison literally threw her into the Afghan's arms and wheeled back in the doorway, lifting the mace. He was as berserk in his own way as was Khoda Khan, frantic with the madness that sometimes inspired men in the midst of combat.

The Mongols came on as if they, too, were blood-mad. They jammed the door with square snarling faces and squat silk-clad bodies before he could slam it shut. Knives licked at him, and gripping the mace with both hands he wielded it like a flail, working awful havoc among the shapes that strove in the doorway, wedged by the pressure from behind. The lights, the upturned snarling faces that dissolved in crimson ruin beneath his flailing, all swam in a red mist. He was not aware of his individual identity. He was only a man with a club, transported back fifty thousand years, a hairy-breasted, red-eyed primitive, wholly possessed in the crimson instinct for slaughter.

He felt like howling his incoherent exultation with each swing of his bludgeon that crushed skulls and spattered blood into his face. He did not feel the knives that found him, hardly realizing it when the men facing him gave back, daunted at the havoc he was wreaking. He did not close the door then; it was blocked and choked by a ghastly mass of crushed and red-dripping flesh.

He found himself running down the corridor, his breath coming in great gulping gasps, following some dim instinct of preservation or realization of duty that made itself heard amidst the red dizzy urge to grip his foes and strike, strike, strike, until he was himself engulfed in the crimson waves of death. In such moments the passion to die—die fighting—is almost equal to the will to live.

In a daze, staggering, bumping into walls and caroming off them, he reached the further end of the corridor where Khoda Khan was struggling with a lock. Joan was standing now, though she reeled on her feet, and seemed on the point of collapse. The mob was coming down the long corridor full cry behind them. Drunkenly Harrison thrust Khoda Khan aside and whirling the blood-fouled mace around his head, struck a stupendous blow that shattered the lock, burst the bolts out of their sockets and caved in the heavy panels as if they had been cardboard. The next instant they were through and Khoda Khan slammed the ruins of the door which sagged on its hinges, but some-how held together. There were heavy metal brackets on each jamb, and Khoda Khan found and dropped an iron bar in place just as the mob surged against it.

Through the shattered panels they howled and thrust their knives, but Harrison knew until they hewed away enough wood to enable them to reach in and dislodge it, the bar across the door would hold the splintered barrier in place. Recovering some of his wits, and feel-ing rather sick, he herded his companions ahead of him with desper-ate haste. He noticed, briefly, that he was stabbed in the calf, thigh, arm and shoulder. Blood soaked his ribboned shirt and ran down his limbs in streams. The Mongols were hacking at the door, snarling like jackals over carrion.

The apertures were widening, and through then he saw other Mongols running down the corridor with rifles; just as he wondered why they did not shoot through the door, then saw the reason. They were in a chamber which had been converted into a magazine. Cartridge cases were piled high along the wall, and there was at least one box of dynamite. But he looked in vain for rifles or pistols. Evidently they were stored in another part of the building.

Khoda Khan was jerking bolts on an opposite door, but he paused to glare about and yelping *"Allah!"* he pounced on an open case, snatched something out—wheeled, yelled a curse and threw back his arm, but Harrison grabbed his wrist.

"Don't throw that, you idiot! You'll blow us all to Hell! They're afraid to shoot into this room, but they'll have that door down in a second or so, and finish us with their knives. Help Joan!"

It was a hand grenade Khoda Khan had found—the only one in an otherwise empty case, as a glance assured Harrison. The detective threw the door open, slammed it shut behind them as they plunged out into the starlight, Joan reeling, half carried by the Afghan. They seemed to have emerged at the back of the house. They ran across an open space, hunted creatures looking for a refuge. There was a crumbling stone wall, about breast-high to a man, and they ran through a wide gap in it, only to halt, a groan bursting from Harrison's lips. Thirty steps behind the ruined wall rose the steel fence of which Khoda Khan had spoken, a barrier ten feet high, topped with keen points. The door crashed open behind them and a gun spat venomously. They were in a trap. If they tried to climb the fence the Mongols had but to pick them off like monkeys shot off a ladder.

"Down behind the wall!" snarled Harrison, forcing Joan behind an uncrumbled section of the stone barrier. "We'll make 'em pay for it, before they take us!"

The door was crowded with snarling faces, now leering in triumph. There were rifles in the hands of a dozen. They knew their victims had no firearms, and could not escape, and they themselves could use rifles without fear. Bullets began to splatter on the stone, then with a long-drawn yell Khoda Khan bounded to the top of the wall, ripping out the pin of the hand grenade with his teeth.

"*La illaha illulah; Muhammad rassoul ullah!*" he yelled, and hurled the bomb—not at the group which howled and ducked, but over their heads, into the magazine!

The next instant a rending crash tore the guts out of the night and a blinding blaze of fire ripped the darkness apart. In that glare Harrison had a glimpse of Khoda Khan, etched against the flame, hurtling backward, arms out-thrown—then there was utter blackness in which roared the thunder of the fall of the house of Erlik Khan as the shattered walls buckled, the beams splintered, the roof fell in and story after story came crashing down on the crumpled foundations.

How long Harrison lay like dead he never knew, blinded, deafened and paralyzed; covered by falling debris. His first realization was that there was something soft under him, something that writhed and whimpered. He had a vague feeling he ought not to hurt this soft something, so he began to shove the broken stones and mortar off him. His arm seemed dead, but eventually he excavated himself and staggered up, looking like a scarecrow in his rags. He groped among the rubble, grasped the girl and pulled her up.

"Joan!" His own voice seemed to come to him from a great distance; he had to shout to make her hear him. Their eardrums had been almost split by the concussion.

"Are you hurt?" He ran his one good hand over her to make sure.

"I don't think so," she faltered dazedly. "What—what happened?"

"Khoda Khan's bomb exploded the dynamite. The house fell in on the Mongols. We were sheltered by that wall; that's all that saved us."

The wall was a shattered heap of broken stone, half covered by rubble—a waste of shattered masonry with broken beams thrust up through the litter, and shards of walls reeling drunkenly. Harrison fingered his broken arm and tried to think, his head swimming.

"Where is Khoda Khan?" cried Joan, seeming finally to shake off her daze.

"I'll look for him." Harrison dreaded what he expected to find. "He was blown off the wall like a straw in a wind."

Stumbling over broken stones and bits of timber, he found the Afghan huddled grotesquely against the steel fence. His fumbling fingers told him of broken bones—but the man was still breathing. Joan came stumbling toward him, to fall beside Khoda Khan and flutter her quick fingers over him, sobbing hysterically.

"He's not like civilized man!" she exclaimed, tears running down her stained, scratched face. "Afghans are harder than cats to kill. If we could get him medical attention he'll live. Listen!" She caught Harrison's arm with galvanized fingers; but he had heard it too—the sputter of a motor that was probably a police launch, coming to investigate the explosion.

Joan was tearing her scanty garments to pieces to staunch the blood that seeped from the Afghan's wounds, when miraculously Khoda Khan's pulped lips moved. Harrison, bending close, caught fragments of words: "The curse of Allah—Chinese dog—swine's flesh—my *izzat*."

"You needn't worry about your *izzat*," grunted Harrison, glancing at the ruins which hid the mangled figures that had been Mongolian terrorists. "After this night's work you'll not go to jail—not for all the Chinamen in River Street."

GRAVEYARD RATS

CHAPTER I
The Head from the Grave

Saul Wilkinson awoke suddenly, and lay in the darkness with beads of cold sweat on his hands and face. He shuddered at the memory of the dream from which he had awakened.

But horrible dreams were nothing uncommon. Grisly nightmares had haunted his sleep since early childhood. It was another fear that clutched his heart with icy fingers—fear of the sound that had roused him. It had been a furtive step—hands fumbling in the dark.

And now a small scurrying sounded in the room—a rat running back and forth across the floor.

He groped under his pillow with trembling fingers. The house was still, but imagination peopled its darkness with shapes of horror. But it was not all imagination. A faint stir of air told him the door that gave on the broad hallway was open. He knew he had closed that door before he went to bed. And he knew it was not one of his brothers who had come so subtly to his room.

In that fear-tense, hate-haunted household, no man came by night to his brother's room without first making himself known.

This was especially the case since an old feud had claimed the eldest brother four days since—John Wilkinson, shot down in the streets of the little hill-country town by Joel Middleton, who had escaped into the post oak grown hills, swearing still greater vengeance against the Wilkinsons.

All this flashed through Saul's mind as he drew the revolver from under his pillow.

As he slid out of bed, the creak of the springs brought his heart into his throat, and he crouched there for a moment, holding his breath and straining his eyes into the darkness.

Richard was sleeping upstairs, and so was Harrison, the city detective Peter had brought out to hunt down Joel Middleton. Peter's room was on the ground floor, but in another wing. A yell for help might awaken all three, but it would also bring a hail of lead at him, if Joel Middleton were crouching over there in the blackness.

Saul knew this was his fight, and must be fought out alone, in the darkness he had always feared and hated. And all the time sounded that light, scampering patter of tiny feet, racing up and down, up and down . . . .

Crouching against the wall, cursing the pounding of his heart, Saul fought to steady his quivering nerves. He was backed against the wall which formed the partition between his room and the hall.

The windows were faint grey squares in the blackness, and he could dimly make out objects of furniture in all except one side of the room. Joel Middleton must be over there, crouching by the old fireplace, which was invisible in the darkness.

But why was he waiting? And why was that accursed rat racing up and down before the fireplace, as if in a frenzy of fear and greed? Just so Saul had seen rats race up and down the floor of the meat-house, frantic to get at flesh suspended out of reach.

Noiselessly, Saul moved along the wall toward the door. If a man was in the room, he would presently be lined between himself and a window. But as he glided along the wall like a night-shirted ghost, no ominous bulk grew out of the darkness. He reached the door and closed it soundlessly, wincing at his nearness to the unrelieved blackness of the hall outside.

But nothing happened. The only sounds were the wild beating of his heart, the loud ticking of the old clock on the mantelpiece—the maddening patter of the unseen rat. Saul clenched his teeth against the shrieking of his tortured nerves. Even in his growing terror he found time to wonder frantically why that rat ran up and down before the fireplace.

The tension became unbearable. The open door proved that Middleton, or someone—or *something*—had come into that room. Why would Middleton come save to kill? But why in God's name had he not struck already? What was he waiting for?

Saul's nerve snapped suddenly. The darkness was strangling him and those pattering rat-feet were red-hot hammers on his crumbling brain. He must have light, even though that light brought hot lead ripping through him.

In stumbling haste he groped to the mantelpiece, fumbling for the lamp. And he cried out—a choked, horrible croak that could not have carried beyond his room. For his hand, groping in the dark on the mantel, had touched the hair on a human scalp!

A furious squeal sounded in the darkness at his feet and a sharp pain pierced his ankle as the rat attacked him, as if he were an intruder seeking to rob it of some coveted object.

But Saul was hardly aware of the rodent as he kicked it away and reeled back, his brain a whirling turmoil. Matches and candles were on the table, and to it he lurched, his hands sweeping the dark and finding what he wanted.

He lighted a candle and turned, gun lifted in a shaking hand. There was no living man in the room except himself. But his distended eyes focused themselves on the mantelpiece—and the object on it.

He stood frozen, his brain at first refusing to register what his eyes revealed. Then he croaked inhumanly and the gun crashed on the hearth as it slipped through his numb fingers.

John Wilkinson was dead, with a bullet through his heart. It had been three days since Saul had seen his body nailed into the crude coffin and lowered into the grave in the old Wilkinson family graveyard. For three days the hard clay soil had baked in the hot sun above the coffined form of John Wilkinson.

Yet from the mantel John Wilkinson's face leered at him—white and cold and dead.

It was no nightmare, no dream of madness. There, on the mantelpiece rested John Wilkinson's severed head.

And before the fireplace, up and down, up and down, scampered a creature with red eyes, that squeaked and squealed—a great grey rat, maddened by its failure to reach the flesh its ghoulish hunger craved.

Saul Wilkinson began to laugh—horrible, soul-shaking shrieks that mingled with the squealing of the grey ghoul. Saul's body rocked to and fro, and the laughter turned to insane weeping, that gave way in turn to hideous screams that echoed through the old house and brought the sleepers out of their sleep.

They were the screams of a madman. The horror of what he had seen had blasted Saul Wilkinson's reason like a blown-out candle flame.

CHAPTER II
Madman's Hate

It was those screams which roused Steve Harrison, sleeping in an upstairs chamber. Before he was fully awake he was on his way down the unlighted stairs, pistol in one hand and flashlight in the other.

Down in the hallway he saw light streaming from under a closed door, and made for it. But another was before him. Just as Harrison reached the landing, he saw a figure rushing across the hall, and flashed his beam on it.

It was Peter Wilkinson, tall and gaunt, with a poker in his hand. He yelled something incoherent, threw open the door and rushed in.

Harrison heard him exclaim: "Saul! What's the matter? What are you looking at—" Then a terrible cry: *"My God!"*

The poker clanged on the floor, and then the screams of the maniac rose to a crescendo of fury.

It was at this instant that Harrison reached the door and took in the scene with one startled glance. He saw two men in nightshirts grappling in the candlelight, while from the mantel a cold, dead, white face looked blindly down on them, and a grey rat ran in mad circles about their feet.

Into that scene of horror and madness Harrison propelled his powerful, thick-set body. Peter Wilkinson was in sore straits. He had dropped his poker and now, with blood streaming from a wound in his head, he was vainly striving to tear Saul's lean fingers from his throat.

The glare in Saul's eyes told Harrison the man was mad. Crooking one massive arm about the maniac's neck, he tore him loose from his victim with an exertion of sheer strength that not even the abnormal energy of insanity could resist.

The madman's stringy muscles were like steel wires under the detective's hands, and Saul twisted about in his grasp, his teeth snapping, beastlike, for Harrison's bull-throat. The detective shoved the clawing, frothing fury away from him and smashed a fist to the madman's jaw. Saul crashed to the floor and lay still, eyes glazed and limbs quivering.

Peter reeled back against a table, purple-faced and gagging.

"Get cords, quick!" snapped Harrison, heaving the limp figure off the floor and letting it slump into a great arm-chair. "Tear that sheet in strips. We've got to tie him up before he comes to. Hell's fire!"

The rat had made a ravening attack on the senseless man's bare feet. Harrison kicked it away, but it squeaked furiously and came charging back with ghoulish persistence. Harrison crushed it under his foot, cutting short its maddened squeal.

Peter, gasping convulsively, thrust into the detective's hands the strips he had torn from the sheet, and Harrison bound the limp limbs with professional efficiency. In the midst of his task he looked up to see Richard, the youngest brother, standing in the doorway, his face like chalk.

"Richard!" choked Peter. "Look! My God! John's head!"

"I see!" Richard licked his lips. "But why are you tying up Saul?"

"He's crazy," snapped Harrison. "Get me some whiskey, will you?"

As Richard reached for a bottle on a curtained shelf, booted feet hit the porch outside, and a voice yelled: "Hey, there! Dick! What's wrong?"

"That's our neighbor, Jim Allison," muttered Peter.

He stepped to the door opposite the one that opened into the hall and turned the key in the ancient lock. That door opened upon a side porch. A tousle-headed man with his pants pulled on over his night-shirt came blundering in.

"What's the matter?" he demanded. "I heard somebody hollerin', and run over quick as I could. What you doin' to Saul—good God Almighty!"

He had seen the head on the mantel, and his face went ashen.

"Go get the marshal, Jim!" croaked Peter. "This is Joel Middleton's work!"

Allison hurried out, stumbling as he peered back over his shoulder in morbid fascination.

Harrison had managed to spill some liquor between Saul's livid lips. He handed the bottle to Peter and stepped to the mantel. He touched the grisly object, shivering slightly as he did so. His eyes narrowed suddenly.

"You think Middleton dug up your brother's grave and cut off his head?" he asked.

"Who else?" Peter stared blankly at him.

"Saul's mad. Madmen do strange things. Maybe Saul did this."

"No! No!" exclaimed Peter, shuddering. "Saul hasn't left the house all day. John's grave was undisturbed this morning, when I stopped by the old graveyard on my way to the farm. Saul was sane when he went to bed. It was seeing John's head that drove him mad. Joel Middleton has been here, to take this horrible revenge!" He sprang up suddenly, shrilling, "My God, he may still be hiding in the house somewhere!"

"We'll search it," snapped Harrison. "Richard, you stay here with Saul. You might come with me, Peter."

In the hall outside the detective directed a beam of light on the heavy front door. The key was turned in the massive lock. He turned and strode down the hall, asking: "Which door is farthest from any sleeping chamber?"

"The back kitchen door!" Peter answered, and led the way. A few moments later they were standing before it. It stood partly open, framing a crack of starlit sky.

"He must have come and gone this way," muttered Harrison. "You're sure this door was locked?"

"I locked all outer doors myself," asserted Peter. "Look at those scratches on the outer side! And there's the key lying on the floor inside."

"Old-fashioned lock," grunted Harrison. "A man could work the key out with a wire from the outer side and force the lock easily. And this is the logical lock to force, because the noise of breaking it wouldn't likely be heard by anybody in the house."

He stepped out onto the deep back porch. The broad back yard was without trees or brushes, separated by a barbed-wire fence from a pasture lot, which ran to a wood-lot thickly grown with post oaks, part of the woods which hemmed in the village of Lost Knob on all sides.

Peter stared toward that woodland, a low, black rampart in the faint starlight, and he shivered.

"He's out there, somewhere!" he whispered. "I never suspected he'd dare strike at us in our own house. I brought you here to hunt him down. I never thought we'd need you to protect us!"

Without replying, Harrison stepped down into the yard. Peter cringed back from the starlight, and remained crouching at the edge of the porch.

Harrison crossed the narrow pasture and paused at the ancient rail fence which separated it from the woods. They were black as only post oak thickets can be.

No rustle of leaves, no scrape of branches betrayed a lurking presence. If Joel Middleton had been there, he must have already sought refuge in the rugged hills that surrounded Lost Knob.

Harrison turned back toward the house. He had arrived at Lost Knob late the preceding evening. It was now somewhat past midnight. But the grisly news was spreading, even in the dead of night.

The Wilkinson house stood at the western edge of the town, and the Allison house was the only one within a hundred yards of it. But Harrison saw lights springing up in distant windows.

Peter stood on the porch, head out-thrust on his long, buzzard-like neck.

"Find anything?" he called anxiously.

"Tracks wouldn't show on this hard-baked ground," grunted the detective. "Just what did you see when you ran into Saul's room?"

"Saul standing before the mantelboard, screaming with his mouth wide open," answered Peter. "When I saw—what he saw, I must have cried out and dropped the poker. Then Saul leaped on me like a wild beast."

"Was his door locked?"

"Closed, but not locked. The lock got broken accidentally a few days ago."

"One more question: has Middleton ever been in this house before?"

"Not to my knowledge," replied Peter grimly. "Our families have hated each other for twenty-five years. Joel's the last of his name."

Harrison re-entered the house. Allison had returned with the marshal, McVey, a tall, taciturn man who plainly resented the detective's presence. Men were gathering on the side porch and in the yard. They talked in low mutters, except for Jim Allison, who was vociferous in his indignation.

"This finishes Joel Middleton!" he proclaimed loudly. "Some folks sided with him when he killed John. I wonder what they think now? Diggin' up a dead man and cuttin' his head off! That's Injun work! I reckon folks won't wait for no jury to tell 'em what to do with Joel Middleton!"

"Better catch him before you start lynchin' him," grunted McVey. "Peter, I'm takin' Saul to the county seat."

Peter nodded mutely. Saul was recovering consciousness, but the mad glaze of his eyes was unaltered. Harrison spoke:

"Suppose we go to the Wilkinson graveyard and see what we can find? We might be able to track Middleton from there."

"They brought you in here to do the job they didn't think I was good enough to do," snarled McVey. "All right. Go ahead and do it—alone. I'm takin' Saul to the county seat."

With the aid of his deputies he lifted the bound maniac and strode out. Neither Peter nor Richard offered to accompany him. A tall, gangling man stepped from among his fellows and awkwardly addressed Harrison:

"What the marshal does is his own business, but all of us here are ready to help all we can, if you want to git a posse together and comb the country."

"Thanks, no." Harrison was unintentionally abrupt. "You can help me by all clearing out, right now. I'll work this thing out alone, in my own way, as the marshal suggested."

The men moved off at once, silent and resentful, and Jim Allison followed them, after a moment's hesitation. When all had gone, Harrison closed the door and turned to Peter.

"Will you take me to the graveyard?"

Peter shuddered. "Isn't it a terrible risk? Middleton has shown he'll stop at nothing."

"Why should he?" Richard laughed savagely. His mouth was bitter, his eyes alive with harsh mockery, and lines of suffering were carven deep in his face.

"We never stopped hounding him," said he. "John cheated him out of his last bit of land—that's why Middleton killed him. For which you were devoutly thankful!"

"You're talking wild!" exclaimed Peter.

Richard laughed bitterly. "You old hypocrite! We're all beasts of prey, we Wilkinsons—like this thing!" He kicked the dead rat viciously. "We all hated each other. You're glad Saul's crazy! You're glad John's dead. Only me left now, and I have a heart disease. Oh, stare if you like! I'm no fool. I've seen you poring over Aaron's lines in 'Titus Andronicus':

"Oft have I digg'd up dead men from their graves,

And set them upright at their dear friends' doors!"

"You're mad yourself!" Peter sprang up, livid.

"Oh, am I?" Richard had lashed himself almost into a frenzy. "What proof have we that you didn't cut off John's head? You knew Saul was a neurotic, that a shock like that might drive him mad! And you visited the graveyard yesterday!"

Peter's contorted face was a mask of fury. Then, with an effort of iron control, he relaxed and said quietly: "You are over-wrought, Richard."

"Saul and John hated you," snarled Richard. "I know why. It was because you wouldn't agree to leasing our farm on Wild River to that oil company. But for your stubbornness we might all be wealthy."

"You know why I wouldn't lease," snapped Peter. "Drilling there would ruin the agricultural value of the land—certain profit, not a risky gamble like oil."

"So you say," sneered Richard. "But suppose that's just a smoke screen? Suppose you dream of being the sole, surviving heir, and becoming an oil millionaire all by yourself, with no brothers to share—"

Harrison broke in: "Are we going the chew the rag all night?"

"No!" Peter turned his back on his brother. "I'll take you to the graveyard. I'd rather face Joel Middleton in the night than listen to the ravings of this lunatic any longer. "

"I'm not going," snarled Richard. "Out there in the black night there's too many chances for you to remove the remaining heir. I'll go and stay the rest of the night with Jim Allison."

He opened the door and vanished in the darkness.

Peter picked up the head and wrapped it in a cloth, shivering lightly as he did so.

"Did you notice how well preserved the face is?" he muttered.

"One would think that after three days—Come on. I'll take it and put it back in the grave where it belongs."

"I'll kick this dead rat outdoors," Harrison began, turning—and then stopped short. "The damned thing's gone!"

Peter Wilkinson paled as his eyes swept the empty floor.

"It was there!" he whispered. "It was dead. You smashed it! It couldn't come to life and run away."

"We'll, what about it?" Harrison did not mean to waste time on this minor mystery.

Peter's eyes gleamed wearily in the candlelight.

"It was a graveyard rat!" he whispered. "I never saw one in an in-habited house, in town, before! The Indians used to tell strange tales about them! They said they were not beasts at all, but evil, cannibal de-mons, into which entered the spirits of wicked, dead men at whose corpses they gnawed!"

"Hell's fire!" Harrison snorted, blowing out the candle. But his flesh crawled. After all, a dead rat could not crawl away by itself.

CHAPTER III
The Feathered Shadow

Clouds had rolled across the stars. The air was hot and stifling. The narrow, rutty road that wound westward into the hills was atrocious. But Peter Wilkinson piloted his ancient Model T Ford skill-fully, and the village was quickly lost to sight behind them. They passed no more houses. On each side the dense post oak thickets crowded close to the barbed-wire fences.

Peter broke the silence suddenly:

"How did that rat come into our house? They overrun the woods along the creeks, and swarm in every country graveyard in the hills.

But I never saw one in the village before. It must have followed Joel Middleton when he brought the head—"

A lurch and a monotonous bumping brought a curse from Harrison. The car came to a stop with a grind of brakes.

"Flat," muttered Peter. "Won't take me long to change tires. You watch the woods. Joel Middleton might be hiding anywhere."

That seemed good advice. While Peter wrestled with rusty metal and stubborn rubber, Harrison stood between him and the nearest clump of trees, with his hand on his revolver. The night wind blew fitfully through the leaves, and once he thought he caught the gleam of tiny eyes among the stems.

"That's got it," announced Peter at last, turning to let down the jack. "We've wasted enough time."

"Listen!" Harrison started, tensed. Off to the west had sounded a sudden scream of pain or fear. Then there came the impact of racing feet on the hard ground, the crackling of brush, as if someone fled blindly through the bushes within a few hundred yards of the road. In an instant Harrison was over the fence and running toward the sounds.

"Help! Help!" it was the voice of dire terror. "Almighty God! Help!"

"This way!" yelled Harrison, bursting into an open flat. The unseen fugitive evidently altered his course in response, for the heavy footfalls grew louder, and then there rang out a terrible shriek, and a figure staggered from the bushes on the opposite side of the glade and fell headlong.

The dim starlight showed a vague writhing shape, with a darker figure on its back. Harrison caught the glint of steel, heard the sound of a blow. He threw up his gun and fired at a venture. At the crack of the shot, the darker figure rolled free, leaped up and vanished in the bushes. Harrison ran on, a queer chill crawling along his spine because of what he had seen in the flash of the shot.

He crouched at the edge of the bushes and peered into them. The shadowy figure had come and gone, leaving no trace except the man who lay groaning in the glade

Harrison bent over him, snapping on his flashlight. He was an old man, a wild, unkempt figure with matted white hair and beard. That beard was stained with red now, and blood oozed from a deep stab in his back.

"Who did this?" demanded Harrison, seeing that it was useless to try to stanch the flow of blood. The old man was dying. "Joel Middleton?"

"It couldn't have been!" Peter had followed the detective. "That's old Joash Sullivan, a friend of Joel's. He's half crazy, but I've suspected that he's been keeping in touch with Joel and giving his tips–"

"Joel Middleton," muttered the old man. "I'd been to find him, to tell the news about John's head–"

"Where's Joel hiding?" demanded the detective.

Sullivan choked on a flow of blood, spat and shook his head.

"You'll never learn from me!" He directed his eyes on Peter with the eerie glare of the dying. "Are you taking your brother's head back to his grave, Peter Wilkinson? Be careful you don't find your own grave before this night's done! Evil on all your name! The devil owns your souls and the graveyard rats'll eat your flesh! The ghost of the dead walks the night!"

"What do you mean?" demanded Harrison. "Who stabbed you?"

"A dead man!" Sullivan was going fast. "As I come back from meetin' Joel Middleton I met him. Wolf Hunter, the Tonkawa chief your grandpap murdered so long ago, Peter Wilkinson! He chased me and knifed me. I saw him plain, in the starlight–naked in his loinclout and feathers and paint, just as I saw him when I was a child, be-fore your grandpap killed him!

"Wolf Hunter took your brother's head from the grave!" Sullivan's voice was a ghastly whisper. "He's come back from Hell to fulfill the curse he laid onto your grandpa when your grandpap shot him in the back, to get the land his tribe claimed. Beware! His ghost walks the night! The graveyard rats are his servants. The graveyard rats—"

Blood burst from his white-bearded lips and he sank back, dead.

Harrison rose somberly.

"Let him lie. We'll pick up his body as we go back to town. We're going on to the graveyard."

"Dare we?" Peter's face was white. "A human I do not fear, not even Joel Middleton, but a ghost—"

"Don't be a fool!" snorted Harrison. "Didn't you say the old man was half crazy?"

"But what if Joel Middleton is hiding somewhere near—"

"I'll take care of him!" Harrison had an invincible confidence in his own fighting ability. What he did not tell Peter, as they returned to the car, was that he had had a glimpse of the slayer in the flash of his shot. The memory of that glimpse still had the short hair prickling at the base of his skull.

That figure had been naked but for a loin-cloth and moccasins and a headdress of feathers.

"Who was Wolf Hunter?" he demanded as they drove on.

"A Tonkawa chief," muttered Peter. "He befriended my grandfa-ther and was later murdered by him, just as Joash said. They say his bones lie in the old graveyard to this day."

Peter lapsed into silence, seemingly a prey of morbid broodings.

Some four miles from town the road wound past a dim clearing. That was the Wilkinson graveyard. A rusty barbed-wire fence surrounded a cluster of graves whose white headstones leaned at crazy angles. Weeds grew thick, straggling over the low mounds.

The post oaks crowded close on all sides, and the road wound through them, past the sagging gate. Across the tops of the trees, nearly half a mile to the west, there was visible a shapeless bulk which Harrison knew was the roof of a house.

"The old Wilkinson farmhouse," Peter answered in reply to his question. "I was born there, and so were my brothers. Nobody's lived in it since we moved to town, ten years ago."

Peter's nerves were taut. He glanced fearfully at the black woods around him, and his hands trembled as he lighted a lantern he took from the car. He winced as he picked up the round cloth-wrapped object that lay on the back seat; perhaps he was visualizing the cold, white, stony face that cloth concealed.

As he climbed over the low gate and led the way between the weed-grown mounds he muttered: "We're fools. If Joel Middleton's laying out there in the woods he could pick us both off easy as shooting rabbits."

Harrison did not reply, and a moment later Peter halted and shone the light on a mound which was bare of weeds. The surface was tumbled and disturbed, and Peter exclaimed: "Look! I expected to find an open grave. Why do you suppose he took the trouble of filling it again?"

"We'll see," grunted Harrison. "Are you game to open that grave?"

"I've seen my brother's head," answered Peter grimly. "I think I'm man enough to look on his headless body without fainting. There are tools in the tool-shed in the corner of the fence. I'll get them."

Returning presently with pick and shovel, he set the lighted lantern on the ground, and the cloth-wrapped head near it. Peter was pale, and sweat stood on his brow in thick drops. The lantern cast their shadows, grotesquely distorted, across the weed-grown graves. The air was oppressive. There was an occasional dull flicker of lightning along the dusky horizons.

"What's that?" Harrison paused, pick lifted. All about them sounded rustlings and scurryings among the weeds. Beyond the circle of lantern light clusters of tiny red beads glittered at him.

"Rats!" Peter hurled a stone and the beads vanished, though the rustlings grew louder. "They swarm in this graveyard. I believe they'd devour a living man, if they caught him helpless. Begone, you servants of Satan!"

Harrison took the shovel and began scooping out mounds of loose dirt.

"Ought not to be hard work," he grunted. "If he dug it out today or early tonight, it'll be loose all the way down—"

He stopped short, with his shovel jammed hard against the dirt, and a prickling in the short hairs at the nape of his neck. In the tense silence he heard the graveyard rats running through the grass.

"What's the matter?" A new pallor greyed Peter's face.

"I've hit solid ground," said Harrison slowly. "In three days, this clayey soil bakes hard as a brick. But if Middleton or anybody else had opened this grave and refilled it today, the soil would be loose all the way down. It's not. Below the first few inches it's packed and baked hard! The top has been scratched, but the grave has never been opened since it was first filled, three days ago!"

Peter staggered with an inhuman cry.

"Then it's true!" he screamed. "Wolf Hunter *has* come back! He reached up from Hell and took John's head without opening the grave! He sent his familiar devil into our house in the form of a rat! A ghost-rat that could not be killed! Hands off, curse you!"

For Harrison caught at him, growling: "Pull yourself together, Peter!"

But Peter struck his arm aside and tore free. He turned and ran—not toward the car parked outside the graveyard, but toward the opposite fence. He scrambled across the rusty wires with a ripping of cloth and vanished in the woods, heedless of Harrison's shouts.

"Hell!" Harrison pulled up, and swore fervently. Where but in the black-hill country could such things happen? Angrily he picked up the tools and tore into the close-packed clay, baked by a blazing sun into almost iron hardness.

Sweat rolled from him in streams, and he grunted and swore, but persevered with all the power of his massive muscles. He meant to prove or disprove a suspicion growing in his mind—a suspicion that the body of John Wilkinson had never been placed in that grave.

The lightning flashed oftener and closer, and a low mutter of thunder began in the west. An occasional gust of wind made the lantern flicker, and as the mound beside the grave grew higher, and the man digging there sank lower and lower in the earth, the rustling in the grass grew louder and the red beads began to glint in the weeds. Harrison heard the eerie gnashings of tiny teeth all about him, and swore at the memory of grisly legends, whispered by the Negroes of his boyhood region about the graveyard rats.

The grave was not deep. No Wilkinson would waste much labor on the dead. At last the rude coffin lay uncovered before him. With the point of the pick he pried up one corner of the lid, and held the lantern close. A startled oath escaped his lips. The coffin was not empty. It held a huddled, headless figure.

Harrison climbed out of the grave, his mind racing, fitting together pieces of the puzzle. The stray bits snapped into place, forming a pattern, dim and yet incomplete, but taking shape. He looked for the cloth-wrapped head, and got a frightful shock.

The head was gone!

For an instant Harrison felt cold sweat clammy on his hands. Then he heard a clamorous squeaking, the gnashing of tiny fangs.

He caught up the lantern and shone the light about. In its reflection he saw a white blotch on the grass near a straggling clump of bushes that had invaded the clearing. It was the cloth in which the head had been wrapped. Beyond that a black, squirming mound heaved and tumbled with nauseous life.

With an oath of horror he leaped forward, striking and kicking. The graveyard rats abandoned the head with rasping squeaks, scattering before him like darting black shadows. And Harrison shuddered. It was no face that stared up at him in the lantern light, but a white, grinning skull, to which clung only shreds of gnawed flesh.

While the detective burrowed into John Wilkinson's grave, the graveyard rats had torn the flesh from John Wilkinson's head.

Harrison stooped and picked up the hideous thing, now triply hideous. He wrapped it in the cloth, and as he straightened, something like fright took hold of him.

He was ringed in on all sides by a solid circle of gleaming red sparks that shone from the grass. Held back by their fear, the graveyard rats surrounded him, squealing their hate.

Demons, the Negroes called them, and in that moment Harrison was ready to agree.

They gave back before him as he turned toward the grave, and he did not see the dark figure that slunk from the bushes behind him. The thunder boomed out, drowning even the squeaking of the rats, but he heard the swift footfall behind him an instant before the blow was struck.

He whirled, drawing his gun, dropping the head, but just as he whirled, something like a louder clap of thunder exploded in his head, with a shower of sparks before his eyes.

As he reeled backward he fired blindly, and cried out as the flash showed him a horrific, half-naked, painted, feathered figure, crouching with a tomahawk uplifted—the open grave was behind Harrison as he fell.

Down into the grave he toppled, and his head struck the edge of the coffin with a sickening impact. His powerful body went limp; and like darting shadows, from every side raced the graveyard rats, hurling themselves into the grave in a frenzy of hunger and blood-lust.

CHAPTER IV
Rats in Hell

It seemed to Harrison's stunned brain that he lay in blackness on the darkened floors of Hell, a blackness lit by darts of flame from the eternal fires. The triumphant shrieking of demons was in his ears as they stabbed him with red-hot skewers.

He saw them, now—dancing monstrosities with pointed noses, twitching ears, red eyes and gleaming teeth—a sharp pain knifed through his flesh.

And suddenly the mists cleared. He lay, not on the floor of Hell, but on a coffin in the bottom of a grave; the fires were lightning flashes from the black sky; and the demons were rats that swarmed over him, slashing with razor-sharp teeth.

Harrison yelled and heaved convulsively, and at his movement the rats gave back in alarm. But they did not leave the grave; they massed solidly along the walls, their eyes glittering redly.

Harrison knew he could have been senseless only a few seconds. Otherwise, these grey ghouls would have already stripped the living flesh from his bones—as they had ripped the dead flesh from the head of the man on whose coffin he lay.

Already his body was stinging in a score of places, and his clothing was damp with his own blood.

Cursing, he started to rise—and a chill of panic shot through him! Falling, his left arm had been jammed into the partly-open coffin, and the weight of his body on the lid clamped his hand fast. Harrison fought down a mad wave of terror.

He would not withdraw his hand unless he could lift his body from the coffin lid—and the imprisonment of his hand held him prostrate there.

Trapped!

In a murdered man's grave, his hand locked in the coffin of a headless corpse, with a thousand grey ghoul-rats ready to tear the flesh from his living frame!

As if sensing his helplessness, the rats swarmed upon him. Harrison fought for his life, like a man in a nightmare. He kicked, he yelled, he cursed, he smote them with the heavy six-shooter he still clutched in his hand.

Their fangs tore at him, ripping cloth and flesh, their acrid scent nauseated him; they almost covered him with their squirming, writhing bodies. He beat them back, smashed and crushed them with blows of his six-shooter barrel.

The living cannibals fell on their dead brothers. In desperation he twisted half-over and jammed the muzzle of his gun against the coffin lid.

At the flash of fire and the deafening report, the rats scurried in all directions.

Again and again, he pulled the trigger until the gun was empty. The heavy slugs crashed through the lid, splitting off a great sliver from the edge. Harrison drew his bruised hand from the aperture.

Gagging and shaking, he clambered out of the grave and rose grog-gily to his feet. Blood was clotted in his hair from the gash the ghostly hatchet had made in his scalp, and blood trickled from a score of tooth-wounds in his flesh. Lightning played constantly, but the lan-tern was still shining. But it was not on the ground.

It seemed to be suspended in mid-air—and then he was aware that it was held in the hand of a man—a tall man in a black slicker, whose eyes burned dangerously under his broad hat-brim. In his other hand a black pistol muzzle menaced the detective's midriff.

"You must be that damn' low-country law Pete Wilkinson brung up here to run me down!" growled this man.

"Then you're Joel Middleton!" grunted Harrison.

"Sure I am!" snarled the outlaw. "Where's Pete, the old devil?"

"He got scared and ran off."

"Crazy, like Saul, maybe," sneered Middleton. "Well, you tell him I been savin' a slug for his ugly mug a long time. And one for Dick, too."

"Why did you come here?" demanded Harrison.

"I heard shootin'. I got here just as you was climbin' out of the grave. What's the matter with you? Who was it that broke your head?"

"I don't know his name," answered Harrison, caressing his aching head.

"Well, it don't make no difference to me. But I want to tell you that I didn't cut John's head off. I killed him because he needed it." The outlaw swore and spat. "But I didn't do that other!"

"I know you didn't," Harrison answered.

"Eh?" The outlaw was obviously startled.

"Do you know which rooms the Wilkinsons sleep in, in their house in town?"

"Naw," snorted Middleton. "Never was in their house in my life."

"I thought not. Whoever put John's head on Saul's mantel knew. The back kitchen door was the only one where the lock could have been forced without waking somebody up. The lock on Saul's door was broken. You couldn't have known those things. It looked like an inside job from the start. The lock was forced to make it look like an outside job.

"Richard spilled some stuff that cinched my belief that it was Peter. I decided to bring him out to the graveyard and see if his nerve would stand up under an accusation across his brother's open coffin. But I hit hard-packed soil and knew the grave hadn't been opened. It gave me a turn and I blurted out what I'd found. But it's simple, after all.

"Peter wanted to get rid of his brothers. When you killed John, that suggested a way to dispose of Saul. John's body stood in its coffin in the Wilkinsons' parlor until it was placed in the grave the next day. No death watch was kept. It was easy for Peter to go into the parlor while his brothers slept, pry up the coffin lid and cut off John's head. He put it on ice somewhere to preserve it. When I touched it I found it was nearly frozen.

"No one knew what had happened, because the coffin was not opened again. John was an atheist, and there was the briefest sort of ceremony. The coffin was not opened for his friends to take a last look, as is the usual custom. Then tonight the head was placed in Saul's room. It drove him raving mad.

"I don't know why Peter waited until tonight, or why he called me into the case. He must be partly insane himself. I don't think he meant to kill me when we drove out here tonight. But when he discovered I knew the grave hadn't been opened tonight, he saw the game was up. I ought to have been smart enough to keep my mouth shut, but I was so sure that Peter had opened the grave to get the head, that when I found it *hadn't* been opened, I spoke involuntarily, without stopping to think of the other alternative. Peter pretended a panic and ran off. Later he sent back his partner to kill me."

"Who's he?" demanded Middleton.

"How should I know? Some fellow who looks like an Indian!"

"That old yarn about a Tonkawa ghost has went to your brain!" scoffed Middleton.

"I didn't say it was a ghost," said Harrison, nettled. "It was real enough to kill your friend Joash Sullivan!"

"What?" yelled Middleton. "Joash killed? Who done it?"

"The Tonkawa ghost, whoever he is. The body is lying about a mile back, beside the road, amongst the thickets, if you don't believe me."

Middleton ripped out a terrible oath.

"By God, I'll kill somebody for that! Stay where you are! I ain't goin' to shoot no unarmed man, but if you try to run me down I'll kill you sure as Hell. So keep off my trail. I'm goin', and don't you try to follow me!"

The next instant Middleton had dashed the lantern to the ground where it went out with a clatter of breaking glass.

Harrison blinked in the sudden darkness that followed, and the next lightning flash showed him standing alone in the ancient graveyard.

The outlaw was gone.

CHAPTER V
The Rats Eat

Cursing, Harrison groped on the ground, lit by the lightning flashes. He found the broken lantern, and he found something else.

Rain drops splashed against his face as he started toward the gate.

One instant he stumbled in velvet blackness, the next the tombstones shone white in the dazzling glare. Harrison's head ached frightfully. Only chance and a tough skull had saved his life. The would-be killer must have thought the blow was fatal and fled, taking John Wilkinson's head for what grisly purpose there was no knowing. But the head was gone.

Harrison winced at the thought of the rain filling the open grave, but he had neither the strength nor the inclination to shovel the dirt back in it. To remain in that dark graveyard might well be death. The slayer might return.

Harrison looked back as he climbed the fence. The rain had disturbed the rats; the weeds were alive with scampering, flame-eyed shadows. With a shudder, Harrison made his way to the flivver. He climbed in, found his flashlight and reloaded his revolver.

The rain grew in volume. Soon the rutty road to Lost Knob would be a welter of mud. In his condition he did not feel able to the task of driving back through the storm over that abominable road. But it could not be long until dawn. The old farmhouse would afford him a refuge until daylight.

The rain came down in sheets, soaking him, dimming the already uncertain lights as he drove along the road, splashing noisily through the mud-puddles. Wind ripped through the post oaks. Once he grunted and batted his eyes. He could have sworn that a flash of lightning had fleetingly revealed a painted, naked, feathered figure gliding among the trees!

The road wound up a thickly wooded eminence, rising close to the bank of a muddy creek. On the summit the old house squatted. Weeds and low bushes straggled from the surrounding woods up to the sagging porch. He parked the car as close to the house as he could get it, and climbed out, struggling with the wind and rain.

He expected to have to blow the lock off the door with his gun, but it opened under his fingers. He stumbled into a musty-smelling room, weirdly lit by the flickering of the lightning through the cracks of the shutters.

His flashlight revealed a rude bunk built against a side wall, a heavy hand-hewn table, a heap of rags in a corner. From this pile of rags black furtive shadows darted in all directions.

Rats! Rats again!

Could he never escape them?

He closed the door and lit the lantern, placing it on the table. The broken chimney caused the flame to dance and flicker, but not enough wind found its way into the room to blow it out. Three doors, leading into the interior of the house, were closed. The floor and walls were pitted with holes gnawed by the rats.

Tiny red eyes glared at him from the apertures.

Harrison sat down on the bunk, flashlight and pistol on his lap. He expected to fight for his life before day broke. Peter Wilkinson was out there in the storm somewhere, with a heart full of murder, and either allied to him or working separately—in either case an enemy to the detective—was that mysterious painted figure.

And that figure was Death, whether living masquerader or Indian ghost. In any event, the shutters would protect him from a shot from the dark, and to get at him his enemies would have to come into the lighted room where he would have an even chance—which was all the big detective had ever asked.

To get his mind off the ghoulish red eyes glaring at him from the floor, Harrison brought out the object he had found lying near the broken lantern, where the slayer must have dropped it.

It was a smooth oval of flint, made fast to a handle with rawhide thongs—the Indian tomahawk of an elder generation. And Harrison's eyes narrowed suddenly; there was blood on the flint, and some of it was his own. But on the other point of the oval there was more blood, dark and crusted, with strands of hair lighter than his, clinging to the clotted point.

Joash Sullivan's blood? No. The old man had been knifed. But someone else had died that night. The darkness had hidden another grim deed. . . .

Black shadows were stealing across the floor. The rats were coming back—ghoulish shapes, creeping from their holes, converging on the heap of rags in the far corner—a tattered carpet, Harrison now saw, rolled in a long compact heap. Why should the rats leap upon that rag? Why should they race up and down along it, squealing and biting at the fabric?

There was something hideously suggestive about its contour—a shape that grew more definite and ghastly as he looked.

The rats scattered, squeaking, as Harrison sprang across the room. He tore away the carpet—and looked down on the corpse of Peter Wilkinson.

The back of the head had been crushed. The white face was twisted in a leer of awful terror.

For an instant Harrison's brain reeled with the ghastly possibilities his discovery summoned up. Then he took a firm grasp on himself, fought off the whispering potency of the dark, howling night, the thrashing wet black woods and the abysmal aura of the ancient hills, and recognized the only sane solution of the riddle.

Somberly he looked down on the dead man. Peter Wilkinson's fright had been genuine, after all. In his blind panic he had reverted to the habits of his boyhood and fled toward his old home—and met death instead of security.

Harrison started convulsively as a weird sound smote his ears above the roar of the storm—the wailing horror of an Indian war-whoop. The killer was upon him!

Harrison sprang to a shuttered window, peered through a crack, waiting for a flash of lightning. When it came he fired through the window at a feathered head he saw peering around a tree close to the car.

In the darkness that followed the flash he crouched, waiting—there came another white glare—he grunted explosively but did not fire. The head was still there, and he got a better look at it. The lightning shone weirdly white upon it.

It was John Wilkinson's fleshless skull, clad in a feathered head-dress and bound in place—and it was the bait of a trap.

Harrison wheeled and sprang toward the lantern on the table. That grisly ruse had been to draw his attention to the front of the house while the killer slunk upon him through the rear of the building! The rats squealed and scattered. Even as Harrison whirled an inner door began to open. He smashed a heavy slug through the panels, heard a groan and the sound of a falling body, and then, just as he reached a hand to extinguish the lantern, the world crashed over his head.

A blinding burst of lightning, a deafening clap of thunder, and the ancient house staggered from gables to foundations! Blue fire crackled from the ceiling and ran down the walls and over the floor. One livid tongue just flicked the detective's shin in passing.

It was like the impact of a sledgehammer. There was in instant of blindness and numb agony, and Harrison found himself sprawling, half-stunned on the floor. The lantern lay extinguished beside the overturned table, but the room was filled with a lurid light.

He realized that a bolt of lightning had struck the house, and that the upper story was ablaze. He hauled himself to his feet, looking for his gun. It lay halfway across the room, and as he started toward it, the bullet-split door swung open. Harrison stopped dead in his tracks.

Through the door limped a man naked but for a loin-cloth and moccasins on his feet. A revolver in his hand menaced the detective. Blood oozing from a wound in his thigh mingled with the paint with which he had smeared himself.

"So it was you who wanted to be the oil millionaire, Richard!" said Harrison.

The other laughed savagely. "Aye, and I will be! And no cursed brothers to share with—brothers I always hated, damn them! Don't move! You nearly got me when you shot through the door. I'm taking no chances with you! Before I send you to Hell, I'll tell you everything.

"As soon as you and Peter started for the graveyard, I realized my mistake in merely scratching the top of the grave—knew you'd hit hard clay and know the grave hadn't been opened. I knew then I'd have to kill you, as well as Peter. I took the rat you mashed when neither of you were looking, so its disappearance would play on Peter's superstitions.

"I rode to the graveyard through the woods, on a fast horse. The Indian disguise was one I thought up long ago. What with that rotten road, and the flat that delayed you, I got to the graveyard before you and Peter did. On the way, though, I dismounted and stopped to kill that old fool Joash Sullivan. I was afraid he might see and recognize me.

"I was watching when you dug into the grave. When Peter got panicky and ran through the woods I chased him, killed him, and brought his body here to the old house. Then I went back after you. I intended bringing your body here, or rather your bones, after the rats finished you, as I thought they would. Then I heard Joel Middleton coming and had to run for it—I don't care to meet that gun-fighting devil anywhere!

"I was going to burn this house with both your bodies in it. People would think, when they found the bones in the ashes, that Middleton killed you both and burnt the house! And now you play right into my hands by coming here! Lightning has struck the house and it's burning! Oh, the gods fight for me tonight!"

A light of unholy madness played in Richard's eyes, but the pistol muzzle was steady, as Harrison stood clenching his great fists helplessly.

"You'll lie here with that fool Peter!" raved Richard. "With a bullet through your head, until your bones are burnt to such a crisp that nobody can tell how you died! Joel Middleton will be shot down by some posse without a chance to talk. Saul will rave out his days in a madhouse! And I, who will be safely sleeping in my house in town before sun-up, will live out my allotted years in wealth and honor, never suspected—never—"

He was sighting along the black barrel, eyes blazing, teeth bared like the fangs of a wolf between painted lips—his finger was curling on the trigger.

Harrison crouched tensely, desperately, poising the hurl himself with bare hands at the killer and try to pit his naked strength against hot lead spitting from that black muzzle—then—

The door crashed inward behind him and the lurid glare framed a tall figure in a dripping slicker.

An incoherent yell rang to the roof and the gun in the outlaw's hand roared. Again, and again, and yet again it crashed, filling the room with smoke and thunder, and the painted figure jerked to the impact of the tearing lead.

Through the smoke Harrison saw Richard Wilkinson toppling—but he too was firing as he fell. Flames burst through the ceiling, and by their brighter glare Harrison saw a painted figure writhing on the floor, a taller figure wavering in the doorway. Richard was screaming in agony.

Middleton threw his empty gun at Harrison's feet.

"Heard the shootin' and come," he croaked. "Reckon that settles the feud for good!" He toppled, and Harrison caught him in his arms, a lifeless weight.

Richard's screams rose to an unbearable pitch. The rats were swarming from their holes. Blood streaming across the floor had dripped into their holes, maddening them. Now they burst forth in a ravening horde that heeded not cries, or movement, or the devouring flames, but only their own fiendish hunger.

In a grey-black wave they swept over the dead man and the dying man. Peter's white face vanished under that wave. Richard's screaming grew thick and muffled. He writhed, half covered by grey, tearing figures who sucked at his gushing blood, tore at his flesh.

Harrison retreated through the door, carrying the dead outlaw. Joel Middleton, outlaw and killer, yet deserved a better fate than was befalling his slayer.

To save that ghoul, Harrison would not have lifted a finger, had it been in his power.

It was not. The graveyard rats had claimed their own. Out in the yard, Harrison let his burden fall limply. Above the roar of the flames still rose those awful, smothered cries.

Through the blazing doorway he had a glimpse of a horror, a gory figure rearing upright, swaying, enveloped by a hundred clinging, tearing shapes. He glimpsed a face that was not a face at all, but a blind, bloody skull-mask. Then the awful scene was blotted out as the flaming roof fell with a thundering, ear-rending crash.

Sparks showered against the sky, the flames rose as the walls fell in, and Harrison staggered away, dragging the dead man, as a storm-wrapped dawn came haggardly over the oak-clad ridges.

BLACK WIND BLOWING

CHAPTER I
"I Take This Woman!"

Emmett Glanton jammed on the brakes of his old Model T and skidded to a squealing stop within a few feet of the apparition that had materialized out of the black, gusty night.

"What the Hell do you mean by jumping in front of my car like that?" he yelled wrathfully, recognizing the figure that posed grotesquely in the glare of the headlights. It was Joshua, the lumbering halfwit who worked for old John Bruckman; but Joshua in a mood such as Glanton had never seen before. In the white glare of the lights the fellow's broad brutish face was convulsed; foam flecked his lips and his eyes were red as those of a rabid wolf. He brandished his arms and croaked incoherently. Impressed, Glanton opened the door and stepped out of the car. On his feet he was inches taller than Joshua, but his rangy, broad-shouldered frame did not look impressive compared to the stooped, apish bulk of the halfwit.

There was menace in Joshua's mien. Gone was the dull, apathetic expression he usually wore. He bared his teeth and snarled like a wild beast as he rolled toward Glanton.

"Keep away from me, blast you!" Glanton warned. "What's the matter with you, anyway?"

"You're goin' over there!" mouthed the halfwit, gesturing vaguely southward. "Old John called you over the phone. I heered him!"

"Yes, he did," answered Glanton. "Asked me to come over as quick as I could. Didn't say why. What about it? You want to ride back with me?"

Joshua jumped up and down and battered his hairy breast like an ape with his splay fists. He gnashed his teeth and howled. Glanton's flesh crawled a little. It was black night, with the wind howling under a black sky, whipping the mesquite. And there in that little spot of light that apish figure cavorted and raved like a witch's familiar summoned up from Hell.

"I don't want to ride with you!" bellowed Joshua. "You ain't goin' there! I'll kill you if you try to go! I'll twist your head off with my hands!" He spread his great fingers and worked them like the hairy legs of great spiders before Glanton's face. Glanton bristled at the threat.

"What are you raving about?" he demanded. "I don't know why Bruckman called me, but—"

"I know!" howled Joshua, froth flying from his loose, working lips. "I listened outside the winder! You can't have her! I want her!"

"Want who?" Glanton was bewildered. This was mystery piled on mystery. Black, howling night, and old John Bruckman's voice shrieking over the party line, edged with frenzy, begging and demanding that his neighbor come to him as quickly as his car could get him there; then the wild drive over the wind-lashed road, and now this lunatic prancing in the glare of the headlights and mouthing bloody threats.

Joshua ignored his question. He seemed to have lost what little sense he had ever had. He was acting like a homicidal maniac. And through the rents in his ragged shirt bulged muscles capable of rending the average man limb from limb.

"I never seen one I wanted before!" he screamed. "But I want her! Old John don't want her! I heered him say so! If you didn't come maybe he'd give her to me! You go on back home or I'll kill you! I'll twist your head off and feed it to the buzzards! You think I'm just a harmless big fool, I bet!"

Grotesquely his bellowing voice rose to a high-pitched squeal.

"Well, if it'll satisfy you," said Glanton, watching him warily, "I've always thought you were dangerous. Bruckman's a fool to keep you on the ranch. I've expected you to go clean crazy and kill him some time."

"I ain't goin' to kill John," howled Joshua. "I'm goin' to kill you. You won't be the first, neither. I killed my brother Jake. He beat me once too often. I beat his head to jelly with a rock and dragged the body down the canyon and throwed it into the pool below the rapids!"

A maniacal glee convulsed his face as he screamed his hideous secret to the night, and his eyes looked like nothing this side of Hell.

"So that's what became of Jake! I always wondered why he disappeared and you came to live with old John. Couldn't stay in your shack in that lonely canyon after you killed him, eh?"

A momentary gleam of fear shot the murk of the maniac's eyes.

"He wouldn't stay in the pool," muttered Joshua. "He used to come back and scratch at the winder, with his head all bloody. I'd wake up at night and see him lookin' in at me and gaspin' and gurglin' tryin' to talk through the blood in his throat.

"But you won't come back and ha'nt me!" he shrieked suddenly, beginning to sway from side to side like a bull about to charge. "I'll spike you down with a stake and weight you down with rocks! I'll—" In the midst of his tirade he lunged suddenly at Glanton.

Glanton knew that if those huge arms ever locked about him his spine would snap like a stick. But he knew, too, that nine times out of ten a maniac will try to reach his victim's throat with his teeth. Joshua was no exception.

Reverting completely to the beast, he plunged in with his arms groping vaguely, and his jaws thrust out like a wolf's muzzle, slavering teeth bared in the glare of the headlights. Glanton stepped inside those waving arms and smashed his right fist against the out-jutting jaw with all his power. It would have stretched another man senseless. It stopped the halfwit in his tracks, and blood spurted.

Before he could recover his balance Glanton struck again and again, raining terrific blows to face and head, driving Joshua reeling and staggering before him. It was like beating a bull, but the ceaseless smashes kept the maniac off balance, confused and dazed him, kept him on the defensive.

Glanton was beginning to tire, and he wondered desperately what the end would be. The moment his blows began weakening Joshua would shake off his bewilderment and lunge to the attack again—

Abruptly they were out of the range of the car lights, and floundering in darkness. In panic lest the maniac should find his throat in the blackness, Glanton swung blindly and desperately, connected glancingly and felt his man fall away from him.

He stumbled himself and went on all fours, almost pitching down the slope that fell away beneath him. Crouching there he heard the sounds of Joshua's thundering fall down the slant. Glanton knew where he was now, knew that a few yards from the road the ground fell away in a steep slope a hundred feet long. It was not hard to navigate by daylight, but by night a man might take a nasty tumble and hurt himself badly on the broken rocks at the bottom. And Joshua, knocked over the edge by Glanton's last wild haymaker, was taking that tumble.

It might have been an animal falling down the slope, from the grunts and howls that welled up from below, but presently, when the rattle of pebbles and the sounds of a heavy rolling body had ceased, there was silence, and Glanton wondered if the lunatic lay senseless or dead at the bottom of the slope.

He called, but there was no answer. Then a sudden shudder shook him. Joshua might be creeping back up the slope in utter silence, this

time maybe with a rock in his hand, such a rock as he had used to bat-
ter his brother Jake's head into a crimson pulp—

Glanton's eyes were getting accustomed to the darkness and he
could make out the vague forms of black ridges, boulders and trees.
The devil-begotten wind that shrieked through the trees would drown
a stealthy footstep. When a man turns his back on peril it assumes an
aspect of thousand-fold horror.

When Glanton started back to the car his flesh crawled cold, and
at each step he expected to feel a frightful form land on his back,
gnashing and tearing. It was with a gasp of relief that he lunged into
the car, eased off the hand-brake, and clattered off down the dim road.

He was leaving Joshua behind him, alive or dead, and such was the
grim magic of the gusty dark that at the moment he feared Joshua
dead no less than Joshua living.

He heaved another sigh of relief when the red spot that was the
light of John Bruckman's house began to glow in the black curtain
ahead of him. He disliked Bruckman, but the old skinflint was sane at
least, and any sane company was welcome after his experience with a
brutish maniac in the black heart of this evil night.

A car stood before Bruckman's gate and Glanton recognized it as
the one belonging to Lem Richards, justice of the peace in Skurlock,
the little village which lay a few miles south of the Bruckman ranch.

Glanton knocked on the door and Bruckman's voice, with a
strange, unnatural quaver in it, shouted:

"Who's there? Speak quick, or I'll shoot through the door!"

"It's me, Glanton!" called the ranchman in a hurry. "You asked me
to come, didn't you?"

Chains rattled, a key grated in the lock, and the door swung inward. The black night seemed to flow in after Glanton with the wind
that made the lamp flicker and the shadows dance along the walls, and

Bruckman moaned and slammed the door in its ebon face. He jammed bolt and chain with trembling hands.

"Your confounded hired hand tried to kill me on the way over," Glanton began angrily. "I've told you that lunatic would go bad some day—"

He stopped short. Two other people were in the room. One was Lem Richards, the justice of the peace, a short, stolid, unimaginative man who sat before the hearth placidly chewing his quid.

The other was a girl, and at the sight of her a sort of shock passed over Emmett Glanton, bringing a sudden realization of his work-hardened hands and hickory shirt and rusty boots. She was like a breath of perfume from the world of tinsel and bright lights and evening gowns that he had almost forgotten in his toil to build up his fortune in this primitive country.

Her supple young figure was set off to its best advantage by the neat but costly dress she wore. Her loveliness dazzled Glanton at first glance; then he looked again and was appalled. For she was white and cold as a statue of marble, and her dilated eyes stared at him as though she had just seen a serpent writhe through the door.

"Oh, excuse me!" he said awkwardly, dragging off, his battered Stetson. "I wouldn't have come busting in here like this if I'd known there was a lady—"

"Never mind that!" snapped John Bruckman. He faced Glanton across the table, his face limned in the lamp-light. It was a haggard face, and in the burning eyes Glanton saw fear, murky bestial fear that made the man repulsive. Bruckman spoke hurriedly, the words tumbling over each other, and from time to time he glanced at the big clock on the mantel sullenly ticking off the seconds.

"Glanton, I hold a mortgage on your ranch, and it's due in a few days. Do you think you can meet your payment?"

Glanton felt like cursing the man. Had he called him over that windswept road on a night like this to discuss a mortgage? A glance at the white, tense girl told him something else was behind all this.

"I reckon I can," he said shortly. "I'm getting by—or would if you'd stay off my back long enough for me to get a start."

"I'll do that!" Bruckman's hands were shaking as he fumbled in his coat. "Look here! Here's the mortgage!" He tossed a document on the table. "And a thousand dollars in cash!" A compact bundle of bank notes plopped down on the table before Glanton's astounded eyes. "It's all yours—mortgage and money—if you'll do one thing for me!"

"And what's that?"

Bruckman's bony forefinger stabbed at the cringing girl.

"Marry her!"

"What?" Glanton wheeled and stared at her with a new intensity, and she stared wildly back, in evident fright, and bewilderment.

"Marry her?" He ran a hand dazedly across his head, vividly aware of the loneliness of the life he had been leading for the past three years.

"What does the young lady think about it?" he asked.

Bruckman snarled impatiently.

"What does it matter what she thinks? She's my niece, my ward. She'll do as I say. She could do worse than marry you. You're no common ridge-runner. You're a gentleman by birth and breeding—"

"Never mind that," growled Glanton, waving him aside. He stepped toward the girl.

"Are you willing to marry me?" he asked directly.

She looked full into his eyes for a long moment, with a desperate and pitiful intensity in her gaze. She must have read kindness and honesty there, for suddenly, impulsively, she sprang forward and caught his brown hand in both of hers, crying:

"Yes! Yes! *Please* marry me! Marry me and take me away from *him*—"

Her gesture toward John Bruckman was one of fear and loathing, but the old man did not heed. He was staring fearfully at the clock again.

He clapped his hands in a spasm of nervousness.

"Quick! Quick! Lem brought the license, according to my instructions. He'll marry you now—now! Stand over here by the table and join hands."

Richards rose heavily and lumbered over to the table, fingering his worn book. All this drama and mystery meant nothing to him, except that another couple were to be married.

And so Emmett Glanton found himself standing holding the quivering hand of a girl he had never seen before, while the justice of the peace mumbled the ritual which made them husband and wife. And only then did he learn the girl's name—Joan Zukor.

"Do you, Emmett, take this woman . . ." droned the monotonous voice.

Glanton gave his reply mechanically, his fingers involuntarily clenching on the slim fingers they grasped. For, pressed briefly against a window, he had seen a face—a white, blood-streaked mask of murder—the face of the halfwit Joshua.

The maniac's eyes burned on Glanton with a mad hate, and on the woman at his side with a sickening flame of desire. Then the face was gone and the window framed only the blackness of the night.

None but Glanton had seen the lunatic. Richards, paid by old John, lumbered stolidly forth and the door shut behind him. Glanton and the girl stood looking at each other speechlessly, in sudden self-consciousness, but old John gave them no pause. He glared at the clock again, which showed ten minutes after eleven, jammed the mortgage and the bank notes into Glanton's hand and pushed him and the girl toward the door. Sweat dripped from his livid face, but a sort of wild triumph mingled with his strange fear.

"Get out! Get off my place! Take your wife and go! I wash my hands of her! I am no longer responsible for her! She's your burden! Go—and go quick!"

CHAPTER II
"Tell Them—In Pity's Name"

In a sort of daze Glanton found himself out on the porch with the girl, and from inside came the sound of drawn bolts and hooked chains. Angrily he took a step toward the door, then noticed the girl shivering beside him, huddling about her a cloak she had snatched as they were evicted.

"Come on, Joan," he said awkwardly, taking her arm. "I think your uncle must be crazy. We'd better go."

He felt her shudder.

"Yes, let us go quickly."

Richards, characteristically, had left the yard gate unfastened. It was flapping and banging in the wind which moaned through the junipers. Glanton groped his way toward the sound, sheltering the cowering girl against the gusts that whipped her cloak about her.

He shivered at the thick-set, cone-shaped outlines of the junipers along the walk. Either of them might be hiding the maniac who had glared through the window. The creature was no longer human; he was a beast of prey, ranging the night.

John Bruckman had given Glanton no chance to warn him of the madman. But Glanton decided he would phone back from his ranch house. They could not loiter there in the darkness, with that skulking fiend abroad.

He half expected to find Joshua crouching in the car, but it was empty, and a feeling of relief flooded him as he turned on the lights and their twin beams lanced the dark. The girl beside him sighed too, though she knew nothing of the death that lurked near them. But she sensed the evil of the night, the menace of the crowding blackness. Even such a dim illumination as this was comforting.

Wordless, Glanton started the car and they began the bumping, jolting ride. He was consumed with curiosity, but hesitated to put the question that itched on his tongue. Presently the girl herself spoke.

"You wonder why my uncle sold me like a slave—or an animal!"

"Don't say that!" exclaimed Glanton in quick sympathy. "You need not—"

"Why *shouldn't* you wonder?" she retorted bitterly. "I can only say—I don't know. He's my only relative, as far as I know. I've seen him only a few times in my life. Ever since I was a small child I've lived in boarding schools and I always understood he was supplying the money that lodged, dressed and educated me. But he seldom wrote; hardly ever visited me.

"I was in a school in Houston when I received a wire from my uncle ordering me to come to him at once. I came on the train to Skurlock, and arrived about nine tonight. Mr. Richards met me at the station. He told me that my uncle had phoned and asked him to drive me out to his ranch. He had the license with him, though I didn't know it at the time.

"When we got here my uncle told me abruptly that I'd have to marry a young man he had sent for. Naturally, I—I was terrified—" She faltered and then laid a timid hand on his arm. "I was afraid—I didn't know what kind of a man it might be."

"I'll be a good husband to you, girl," he said awkwardly, and thrilled with pleasure at the sincerity in her tone as she replied:

"I know it. You have kind eyes and gentle hands. Strong, but gentle."

They were approaching a place where the road had been straightened by a new track, which, instead of swinging wide around the sloping edge of a steep, thicket-grown knoll, crossed a shallow ravine by a crude bridge and ran close by the knob on the opposite side, where it sheered off in a forty-foot cliff.

As the knoll grew dimly out of the windy darkness ahead of them, a grisly premonition rose in Glanton's breast. Joshua, loping through the mesquite like a lobo wolf, could have reached that knob ahead of them. It was the most logical place along the road for an ambush. A man crouching on the thicket-clad crest of the cliff could hurl a boulder down on a car passing along the new stretch of road—

With sudden decision, Glanton wrenched the car into the old track, now a faint trace grown up in broom weeds and prickly pears.

Joan caught at him for support as she was thrown from side to side by the jouncing of the auto. Then as they swung around the slope and came back into the plain road again, behind and above them yammered a fiendish howling—the maddened, primordial shrieking of a baffled beast of prey which realizes that his victims have eluded him.

"What's that?" gasped Joan, clutching at Glanton.

"Just a bobcat squalling in the brush on that knob," he assured her, but it was with convulsive haste that he jammed his foot down on the accelerator and sent the car thundering down the road. Tomorrow, he swore, he'd raise a posse and hunt down that slavering human beast as he would a rabid coyote.

He could imagine the madman loping along the road after them, foam from his bared fangs dripping onto his bare, hairy breast. He was glad the lamp was burning in the parlor of his ranch house. It reached a warm shaft of light to them across the windy reaches of the night.

He did not drive the car into the shed that served as garage. He drove it as close to the porch as he could get it, and opened the car door in the light that streamed from the house, as old Juan Sanchez, his Mexican man-of-all-work, opened the front door.

Glanton was briefly aware of the bareness of his residence. There had been no time to adorn it in his toil to build his spread. But now he must have a front yard with a fence around it and some rose bushes and spineless decorative cacti. Women liked things like that.

"This is my wife, Sanchez," he said briefly. "Senora Joan."

The old Mexican hid his astonishment with a low bow, and said, with the natural courtliness of his race:

"*Buenas noches, senora!* Welcome to the *hacienda*."

"In the parlor Glanton said: "Sit down by the fire and warm yourself, Joan. It's been a cold drive. Sanchez, stir up the fire and throw on some more mesquite chunks. I'm going to call up John Bruckman. There's something he ought to know—"

But even as he reached for the phone the bell jangled discordantly. As he lifted the receiver over the line came John Bruckman's voice, brittle with fear and more than fear—with physical agony.

"Emmett! Emmett Glanton! Tell them—in pity's name tell them that you've married Joan Zukor! Tell them I'm no longer responsible for her!"

"Tell who?" demanded Glanton, all but speechless with amazement.

Joan was on her feet, white-faced; that frantic voice shrieking from the receiver had reached her ears.

"These devils!" squalled the voice of John Bruckman. "The Black Brothers of—aaagh—Mercy!"

The voice broke in a loud shriek, and in the brief silence that followed there sounded a low, gurgling, indescribably repellent laugh. And Glanton's hair stood up, for he knew it was not John Bruckman who laughed.

"Hello!" he yelled. "John! John Bruckman!"

There was no answer. A click told him that the receiver had been hung up at the other end, and a grisly conviction shook him that it had not been John Bruckman's hand who had hung it up.

He turned to the girl, who stood silent and wide-eyed in the middle of the room, as he snatched a gun from its scabbard hanging on the wall.

"I've got to go back to Bruckman's ranch," he said. "Something devilish is happening over there, and the old man seems to need help bad."

She was speechless. Impulsively he took her hands in his and stroked them reassuringly.

"Don't be afraid, kid," he said. "Sanchez will take care of you till I get back. And I won't be gone long."

CHAPTER III
Dead Madness

As he drew the old Mexican out onto the porch a glance back showed her still standing dumbly in the center of the room, her hands pressed childishly to her breasts, an image of youthful fright and bewilderment lost in an unfamiliar world of violence and horror.

"I don't know what the Hell's happened over at Bruckman's," he said swiftly and low-voiced to Sanchez. "But be careful. Joshua, the halfwit's gone on the rampage. He tried to kill me tonight, and he laid for us at the knob where the new road passes. Probably meant to brain me with a rock and kidnap Joan. Shoot him like a coyote if he shows his head on this ranch while I'm gone."

"Trust me, *senor!*" Old Sanchez's face was grim as he fondled the worn butt of his old single-action Colt. Men had died before that black muzzle in the wild old days when Sanchez had ridden with Pancho Villa. Sanchez could be depended on. Glanton clapped him on the back, leaped into the Ford and roared away southward.

The road before him was a white crack in a black wall, opening steadily in the glare of the headlights. He drove recklessly, half expecting each moment to see the shambling figure of the maniac spring out of the blackness. Grimly he touched the butt of the pistol thrust into the waistband of his trousers.

Aversion to driving under that gloomy cliff was so strong in Glanton that again he swung aside and followed the dimmer, longer road that wound around the opposite side of the knob.

And as he did so he was aware of another roar, above that of his own racing motor. He caught the reflection of powerful headlights. Some other car was eating up the road, racing northward and taking the shorter cut. As he drove into the open road beyond the knob he looked back and glimpsed a rapidly receding tail-light. A nameless foreboding seized him, urging him to wheel around and race back to his own ranch.

But there was not necessarily anything sinister in a car speeding northward even at that hour. It was probably some ranchman who lived north of Glanton returning home from Skurlock, or some traveling salesman bound for one of the little cowtowns still further north, and leaving the paved highways to take a short cut.

There was no light in the window of the Bruckman ranch house as Glanton approached it; only the glow of the fire in the fireplace staining the windows with lurid blood, crimsoning it without illuminating. There was no sound but the moaning of the ghostly wind through the dark junipers as Glanton went up the walk. But the front door stood open.

Pistol in hand, Glanton peered in. He caught the glimmer of red coals glowing on the hearth. The dry, toneless ticking of the clock made him start nervously.

He called: "John! John Bruckman!"

No answer, but somewhere a moan rose in the fire-shadowed darkness, a low, whimpering of anguish, thick and gurgling as if through a gag of welling blood. And a steady drip, drip of something wet and sticky on the floor.

Panic clawed at Glanton's spine as he moved toward the smoldering hearth, instinct drawing him toward the one spot of light in the room. At the moment he did not remember just where stood the table with the oil lamp on it. He must have a moment to gather his wits, to locate it.

He groped for a match, then froze in his tracks. A black hand had materialized out of the shadows, faintly revealed in the light of the glowing embers. It cast something on the coals while Glanton stood transfixed.

Little tongues of red grew to life; the fire rose and the shadows retreated before the widening pool of wavering light. A face grew out of the darkness before Emmett Glanton—a grinning face that was like a carven mask somehow imbued with evil life. White pointed teeth reflected the firelight, eyes red as the eyes of an owl burned at him.

With a choking cry Glanton lifted his gun and fired full at the face. At that range he could not miss. The face vanished with a shattering crash and Glanton was showered with tiny particles that stung his hand.

But a low laugh rang through the room—the laugh he had heard over the phone! Whence it came he could not be sure, but in the flash of intuition that came to him, as it often comes to men in desperate straits, he realized the trick that had been played upon him, and wheeled with a gasp of pure terror. Pointblank he fired, with the muzzle jammed against the bulk that was almost on him—the bulk of the fiend that had crept up *behind him while he was staring at its reflection in front of him.*

There was an agonized grunt and something that swished venomously ripped away the front of his shirt. And then the monster was down and floundering in its death throes in the shadows at his feet, and in a panic Glanton fired down at it again and again, until its thrashing ceased and in the deafening silence that followed the booming of the shots he heard only the dry tick-tock of the clock, the drip-drip on the floor and the moaning that rose eerily in the gruesome dark.

His hands were clammy with sweat when he found the oil lamp and lighted it. As the flame sprang up, sending the shadows slinking back to the corners, he glared fearfully at the thing sprawled before the hearth. At least it was a *man*—a tall, powerful man, naked to the waist, his shoulders and arching chest gigantic, his arms thick with knotting muscles.

Blood oozed from three wounds in that massive torso. He was black, but he was not a Negro. He seemed to be stained with some sort of paint from his shaven crown to his fingertips. And the fingers of one hand were frightfully armed, with steel hooks that were hollow nearly to the points and slipped over the fingers, curving and razor sharp, making terrible, tiger-like talons.

The thick lips, drawn back, revealed teeth filed to points, and then Glanton saw that he was not painted all over, after all. In the center of the breast a circle of white skin showed, and inside that circle there was a strange black symbol; it looked like a blind, black face.

An arrangement of mirrors fastened at right angles to the mantel and to the wall, one shattered by his bullet, revealed the trick by which he meant to take Glanton off guard. He must have made his arrangements, simple and easy enough, when he heard the car driving up. But it was diabolical, betraying a twisted mind.

From where he had been standing, Glanton could not see his own reflection in the mirror on the mantel, but only the reflection of the black man behind and to one side of him, like a spectral face floating in the shadows.

What takes long in the telling flashed lightning-like through Glanton's mind as he looked down at the black man; and then he saw something else. He saw old John Bruckman.

The old man lay naked on a table, on his back, arms and legs spread wide, so that his body formed a St. Andrew's Cross. Through each hand, nailing it to the wood, and through each ankle, a black spike had been driven.

His tongue had been pulled out of his mouth and a steel skewer was driven through it. A ghastly raw, red patch showed on his breast, where a portion of skin as big as a man's palm had been savagely sliced away. And that piece of skin lay on the table beside him and Glanton gasped at the sight of it. For it bore the same unholy symbol that showed on the breast of the dead man by the hearth. Blood trickled along the table, dripped on the floor.

Nauseated, Glanton drew forth the skewer from John Bruckman's tongue. Bruckman gagged, spat forth a great mouthful of blood and made incoherent sounds.

"Take it easy, John," said Glanton. "I'll get some pliers and pull these spikes out—"

"Let them be!" gurgled Bruckman, scarcely intelligible with his butchered tongue. "They're barbed—you'll tear my hands off. I'm dying—they hurt me in ways that don't show so plainly. Let me die in as little pain as possible. Sorry—would have warned you *he* was waiting for you in the dark—but this accursed skewer—couldn't even scream.

He heard your car and made ready—mirrors—always carry their paraphernalia with them—paraphernalia of illusion—deception and murder! Whiskey, quick! On that shelf!"

Though he winced at the sting of the fiery liquid on his mangled tongue, Bruckman's voice grew stronger; and a blaze rose in his bloodshot eyes.

"I'm going to tell you everything," he panted. "I'll live that long—then you set the law on them—blast them off the earth! I've kept the oath until now, even with the threat of death hanging over me, but I thought I could fool them. Curse their black souls, I'll keep their secret no longer! Don't talk or ask questions—listen!"

Strange the tales that dying lips have gasped, but never a stranger tale than that Emmett Glanton heard in the blood-stained room, where a dead black face grinned by a smoldering hearth, and a dying man, spiked to a table, mouthed grisly secrets with a mangled tongue in the smoky light of the guttering lamp, while the black wind moaned and crawled at the rattling windows.

"When I was young, in another land," panted John Bruckman, "I was a fool. And I was trapped by my own folly into joining a cult of devil worshippers—the Black Brothers of Ahriman. Until too late I did not realize what they were—nor to what horrors my own terrible oath had bound me. I need not speak of their aims and purposes—they were foul beyond conception. Yet they had one characteristic that is so often lacking in many such cults—they were sincere—fanatic. They worshipped the fiend Ahriman as zealously as did their heathen ancestors. And they practiced human sacrifice. Once each year, on this very night, between midnight and dawn, a young girl was offered up on the burning altar of Ahriman, Lord of Fire. On that glowing altar her body was consumed to ashes and the ashes scattered to the night wind by the black-painted priests.

"I became one of the Black Brothers. On my breast was tattooed indelibly the symbol of Ahriman, which is the symbol of Night—a blind, black face. But at last I sickened of the revolting practices of the cult, and fled from it. I came to America and changed my name. Some of my people were already here—the branch of the family to which Joan belongs.

"With the passing of nineteen years I thought the Black Brothers had forgotten me. I didn't know there were branches in America, in the teeming foreign quarters of the great cities. But I might have known they never forget. And one day I received a cryptic message that shattered my illusions. They had remembered, had traced me, found me—knew all about me. And, in punishment for my desertion, they had chosen my niece, Joan, for the yearly sacrifice.

"That was bad enough, but what nearly drove me mad with terror was knowledge of the custom that attends the sacrifice—since time immemorial it's been the habit of the Black Brothers to kill the man nearest the girl chosen for sacrifice—father, brother, husband—her 'master' according to their ritual. This is partly because of a dim phallic superstition, partly a practical way of eliminating an enemy, for the girl's protector would certainly seek vengeance.

"I knew I couldn't save Joan. She was marked for doom, but I might save myself by shifting responsibility for her to somebody else's shoulders. So I brought her here and married her to you."

"You swine!" whispered Glanton.

"It did me little good!" gasped Bruckman, his tortured head tossing from side to side. His eyes were glazing and a bloody froth rose to his livid lips. "They came shortly after you drove away. I was fool enough to let them in—told them I was no longer responsible for the chosen maiden. They laughed at me—tortured me. I broke away—got to the phone—but they had ordered my death, as a renegade brother.

They drove away, leaving one of them here to attend to me. You can see he did his work well!"

"Where—where did they go?" Glanton spoke with dry lips, remembering the big automobile roaring northward.

"To your ranch—to get Joan—I told them where she was—before they started torturing me!"

"You fool! You're telling me this *now*," Glanton yelled.

But John Bruckman did not hear, for, with a convulsion that spattered foam from his empurpled lips and tore one of the bloody spikes out of the wood, the life went out of him in one great cry.

CHAPTER IV
Crackling Blue Flame

Like a drunken man, Emmitt Glanton left from that lamp-lit room where a black face on the floor grinned blindly at a blind white face lolling on the table. The black wind ripped at him with mad, invisible fingers as he ran in great leaps to his car.

The drive through the screaming darkness was nightmare, with the black wall splitting before him, and closing behind him, horror hounding him like a werewolf on his trail, and the wind howling awful secrets in his ears.

He did not turn aside for the somber knoll this time, but plunged straight on, thundered over the bridge and rushed past the black cliff. No boulder fell from above. Joshua must have left his ambush long ago.

Three more miles and his heart leaped into his throat and stuck there, a choking chunk of ice. He should be able to see the light in the ranch house window by now—but only the glare of his own headlights knifed the black curtain before him.

Then the ranch house bulked out of the night and on the porch he saw a strange pale spot of radiance glowing. There was no sign of the automobile that had come northward. But he checked his own car suddenly to avoid running over a shape that sprawled in the fenceless yard. It was the mad Joshua, lying face down, one side of his head a mass of blood. He had come only to meet death.

Glanton slid out of the car and ran toward the house, shouting Sanchez' name. His cries died away in the stormy clamor of the wind and an icy hand gripped his heart.

His dilated eyes were fixed on the pale spot that grew in size and shape as he approached—a man's face stared at him—the face of Sanchez, weirdly illuminated. Glanton stole closer, holding his breath. Why should the face of Sanchez glow so in the darkness? Why should he stand so still, unanswering, eyes fixed and glassy? Why should his face be looking down from such a height?

Then Glanton knew. He was looking at Sanchez' severed head, fastened by its long hair to a pillar of the porch. Some sort of phosphorus had been rubbed on the dead face to make that eerie glow.

"Joan!"

It was a cry of agony as Glanton flung himself into the darkened house. Only the wind outside answered him, mocked him. His foot struck something heavy and yielding just inside the door. Sick with horror he found a match and struck it. Near the door lay a headless body, riddled with bullets. It was the body of Sanchez. And but for the corpse the house was empty. The match burned down to Glanton's fingers and he stumbled out of the house.

Out in the yard he fought down hysteria and forced himself to look at the matter rationally. Joshua must have been shot by Sanchez, while trying to sneak up on the house. Then it would have been easy for strangers to catch the old Mexican off-guard. He had not expected an attack from anyone except the halfwit, nor would he have been expecting enemies to come in a motor car. He would have come to the door at a hail from a stopping auto, unsuspectingly showing himself in the lighted doorway. A sudden hail of bullets would have done the rest. And then—beads of perspiration broke out on his body. Joan, alone and undefended, with those fiends!

He whirled, gun in hand, as he thought he heard a noise like something moving in the bushes north of the house. It diminished, ceased as he went in that direction. It might have been a steer, or some smaller beast. It might—suddenly he turned and strode toward the car.

The body that had lain there before was gone. Had dead Joshua risen and stalked away in the shadows, and was it he that Glanton had heard stealing northward through the bushes? Glanton did not greatly care. At that moment he was ready to believe any grisliness was possible, and he had no interest in Joshua, dead or alive.

He walked around the house, wiping the sweat from his face with clammy hands. The house stood on a rise. From it he could see the lights of any car fleeing northward, for several miles. He strained his eyes, but saw no distant shaft splitting the dark. The raiders must have already put many miles between them and the scene of their crimes. He must follow—but where? Northward, yes—but a few miles north of his ranch the road split into three forks, each leading eventually into a highway, one of which ran to New Mexico, one to Oklahoma, and one north into the Panhandle.

He twisted his fingers together in an agony of indecision. Then he stiffened.

He had seen a light—yet not a distinct shaft like a car light. This was more like a blur in the dark—like the glow of embers not yet extinguished. It seemed to emanate from a spot somewhat east of the road which ran north, and this side of the forks. Night made sight and judgment deceptive, but tracing out that eerie glow was better than sitting in racking inaction.

Fixing the spot in his mind as well as he could, he ran to his car and drove northward. As soon as he had descended the rise on which his house stood he could no longer see the glare, but he drove on until he reached a spot which he believed was the point where the road most closely approached the spot where he had seen the glow. A long wooded ridge stood east of the road at that spot.

He left the car and toiled up the western slope of the ridge, scratching his hands and tearing his clothing on rocks and bushes. And nearly to the crest he heard something that stopped him in his tracks. The wind had dwindled to a fitful moaning, and somewhere ahead of him there rose a weird sound that set his flesh crawling.

Chanting! Beyond that black ridge men were chanting in an evil monotone that brought up shuddersome racial memories, old as time and dim as nightmares, of grim black temples where clouds of foul incense smoke rolled about the feet of bowing worshippers before a blood-stained altar. In a frenzy Glanton charged to the crest, tearing through the thickets by sheer force.

Crouching there he looked down on a scene that wrenched his horrified mind back a thousand years into the black night of the medieval when madness stalked the earth in the guise of men.

At the foot of the ridge, in a wide, natural basin glowed a ring of fire. He saw its apparent source—boulders had been rolled to form a solid circle and these boulders glowed with a blue-white light that was like an icy heat beyond human comprehension. From them rose a glow that hung like an unholy halo above the shallow basin. It was this light he had seen from his ranch. It might have been a glow from the slag-heaps of Hell. And devils were not lacking. He saw them, three of them inside the circle—tall, muscular men, naked, black as the night that surrounded them, their heads hidden by grinning golden masks made like the faces of beasts.

They stood about a heap of stones which glowed with a dull blue radiance, and on that crude improvised altar lay a slender, white, unmoving figure.

Glanton almost screamed aloud at the sight. Joan lay there, stark naked, spread-eagled in the form of St. Andrew's Cross, her wrists and ankles strapped securely. In that instant Glanton knew what it would mean to him to lose that girl—realized how much she had come to mean to him in the few hours he had known her. His wife! Even at this moment the phrase brought a strange, warm thrill. And now those devils down there were preparing, by some hellish art, to reduce that lovely body into ashes—

Madly he hurled himself down the slope, pistol in hand. As he went he heard the chanting cease, and was aware of a strange, yet curiously familiar humming in the air.

Whence it came he could not tell, but it sounded like the pulsing of a giant dynamo. Joan cried out. An edge of pain vibrated through her voice.

The halo over the circle mounted, grew more intensely blue. The rocks glowed with a fiercer light; pale tongues of flame licked up from them. The hue of the altar under the girl was changing. The blue was growing more pronounced, less dull. That the change in its color was accompanied by painful sensations was evident from Joan's cries and the writhings of her bound body.

Glanton yelled incoherently as his feet hit level ground, and the black men turned quickly toward him. His lips drew back in a wolfish snarl and the old single-action gun went up in a menacing arc as he thumbed back the fanged hammer. He meant to shoot these devils down in their tracks, like so many mad dogs—then his out-thrust left hand touched one of the glowing boulders. Merely touched it, but the contact was like the jolt of a fork of lightning. Glanton was knocked off his feet and rolled, blind and dizzy with brief but stunning agony. As he staggered up, snarling and still gripping his gun, he recognized the truth.

Somehow those boulders had been made conductors of electricity. They were charged with a voltage terrific beyond his understanding. And so was the altar, though as yet the full force had not been turned on.

The rising hum that now filled the air told its own grisly tale. Joan was to die by electricity, not swiftly shocked to death as in an electric chair, but slowly agonizedly, burned to a crisp—to white ashes to be scattered to the night wind.

With an inhuman yell he threw up his gun and fired. One of the masked men spun on his heels and fell sprawling, but the taller of the remaining two bent quickly and laid a hand on some sort of contraption at his feet.

Instantly the hum grew to a shriek. White fire danced around the ring, blinding and dazzling the man outside. He saw the tall black forms within it vaguely, through a dizzying blue-white curtain of flame.

Shielding his eyes from the glare, panic tugging at his soul, he fired again and again until the hammer fell with an empty snap. He could not hit them. The noise, the glare, bewildered him; everything was thrown out of its proper proportions; vision and perspective were distorted.

He hurled the gun at them and reeled toward the blazing barricade with his bare hands, knowing that to touch it would be death, yet choosing death rather than standing by and watching the girl die. But before he reached it a black shape hurtled past him, out of the darkness. Joshua! Blood clotted his scalp, but his primitive fury, his mad desire for the white body on that glowing altar were undimmed.

Like a charging bull he came out of the dark, headlong at the barrier. Running hard and low he bent, gathered his thews and leaped! Only a beast or a madman could have made that leap. He cleared the barrier with a foot to spare; one instant he was etched in mid-air, black against the glare, arms wide and fingers spread like talons, then he hit catlike on his feet within the ring of death.

And as he struck he lunged. The priests were naked and weaponless. The taller let go the lever he held, sprang aside, stooped and snatched up some object, even as Joshua struck his companion. It might have been a bull that smote and tossed the black priest.

Plain above the lessening hum and crackle of blue flame sounded the snap of splintering bones, the shriek of the priest. He was whirled from his feet, a broken, dangling doll, lifted high in apelike arms above the bullet-head and dashed head first to the earth with such fury that the broken corpse rebounded before it lay still. Head down, the killer plunged at the taller priest's throat.

It had been a pistol this man had snatched up, and a raking blast of lead met the charging madman—met him, but did not stop him.

With bullets smacking into his body at close range, Joshua bellowed with pain and swayed on his feet, but came on in an irresistible surge of fury and threw his arms about the black body of his foe. He must have been dying even then, but the blind force of his rush was enough to carry the priest off his feet. Together they hurtled on—to crash full against the blazing ring of boulders!

A crack like a clap of thunder, a blinding spray of blue fire, one awful scream—then the reek of burnt flesh filled the air. In the swiftly dying glare, Emmett Glanton saw two hideous figures—*both* black now—crumpled in a fused, indistinguishable mass against the dulling rocks.

Something had happened to the generator of that terrible power. The hum had ceased; the demon halo was dying. Already the stones of the altar had assumed their natural tint. But on it the girl lay limp.

As Glanton crawled over the barrier his heart was in his mouth. Tenderly he freed her and lifted her, grateful to feel warm, living flesh under his hands, but setting his teeth against what he might find—but her tender back and limbs showed none of the ghastly burns he feared.

Obviously no great amount of electricity had been turned into the altar. He saw wires running in all directions from the amazingly small, compact, black case-like thing that stood near the altar.

Before he carried Joan out of the ring he smashed the thing with a heavy rock. The Black Brothers knew secrets that were better kept from the world at large. Even clean science became hurtful black magic in their hands. That tiny dynamo, of a type undreamed of by the world, contained more energy than sane men conceived of—power to turn naked rocks into live wires. Such a secret could only be evil.

He whipped off his torn shirt and wrapped the girl in it, as carefully he carried her down to the road.

As he went, he thought of Joshua, and the only logical explanation offered itself. The bullet that had struck the madman had not killed him, but only creased him and knocked him out. When he came to himself, he started on the trail of the woman his crazed brain desired, drawn either by the same glimpse of the distant fire that had drawn Glanton, or by dark, psychic instinct.

Glanton had almost reached the car when Joan opened her eyes, stared about her wildly, then clung to him.

"It's all right, kid," he soothed her. "You're not hurt. You just fainted. Everything's all right now. Joshua paid his debt, without meaning to, poor devil. Look, it's getting daylight. The night's past."

He meant it in more than its literal sense. "Take me home, Emmett," she whimpered, nestling deep into his arms. Then, irrelevantly: "Kiss me."

And Emmett Glanton kissed his wife for the first time, just as dawn touched the eastern hills.